The Blame Lies

By Val Wise

To June
Best wishes
Val Wise

December 2021

ISBN: 9798751284039

Author's Note

Although the public events described in this novel actually occurred between the years 1745 and 1867, I have placed some real characters into fictional situations based on research and reading Harriet's letters preserved in the archives of Beverley Treasure House. However, I have no reason to suspect that Elizabeth Taylor was anything other than a kind, God-fearing woman and Rev. Coltman a well-respected cleric. Little was written about females in the past; they were generally presumed to be passive spectators at significant historical events. But could a woman have been the real culprit? Would she allow others to be falsely accused? That would be when the blame lies.

The cover is part of a reproduction of a coloured engraving depicting the Peterloo Massacre in 1819 by Richard Carlie.

Preface

"Who can tell whether getting everything off my chest will help ease my mind and relieve me of the terrible responsibility of being the only one in this world to know where the real blame lies?"

It is 1862 and Elizabeth Welburn has decided to share the secrets of her amazing life with you. She trusts you not to tell anyone about her involvement in the many scandals that outraged English society over the past forty years. Her acquaintance with people like Sarah Siddons, Georgiana, Duchess of Carlisle, Richard Sheridan, George Canning, Henry Hunt and John Bellingham, the man hung for the murder of the Prime Minister, are all part of this fascinating story.

A humdrum, small town life was never what Elizabeth contemplated. Happily, a travelling theatre company brought her opportunities to attain status in her own right. After often being let down by the men in her life, she learned to use her powers of persuasion to get what she wanted from them. At the time of writing, she is satisfied she can be recognised as a benevolent and successful member of society, but how did she manage that?

As a single middle-class woman, she perceives events of the nineteenth century quite differently from your usual upper-class male historians.

Chapters

1	In which Mrs. J. Welburn becomes a Benefactor of Beverley	1
2	Which treats of Elizabeth Taylor's early life	11
3	Miss Hannah Murphy becomes an esteemed actress	16
4	Melodrama	24
5	An account of the duel between Mr. George Canning and Lord Castlereagh	32
6	A Fire and a Sad Farewell to London	43
7	In which Mr. John Bellingham's story is told	51
8	A Description of Domestic Life	59
9	How Mr. Henry Hunt Became a National Hero	73
10	In Which the Case is Made in Favour of Bribery	89
11	Miss Harriet Fox Widens Her Horizons	97
12	The Election of the Whig Member for Beverley	101
13	London Diversions	105
14	Farewell to Miss Harriet Fox	114

15	Death, Destruction and Deviance	120
16	A History of Reverend Joseph Coltman, the Heaviest Man in England	125
17	Coronation and Calamity	129
18	The Weddings of Mr. and Mrs. John Welburn and also of Queen Victoria	137
19	The Railway King	147
20	Where the Blame Really Lies	153
	About the Author	160
	Also by Val Wise	161

The Blame Lies

By Val Wise

Chapter 1

In Which Mrs. John Welburn Becomes a
Benefactor of Beverley

Here I am, standing in my bedroom, the cheval mirror reflecting this complacent woman recently returned from a grand dinner at the Hall Garth Inn, smelling faintly of lavender and sherry wine. Who would you see? An inoffensive old woman well past her usefulness? Then no, let me tell you, you would be quite wrong, I am someone who has lived their life like no one else, shaped by most peculiar circumstances.

I promise you I am only slightly befogged; it was good food and the wine really flowed. Mr. Straker the landlord had always put himself out for me and Mr. Welburn; ever glad of a chance to increase his takings it must be said. Just look at the way he looks after those hoggish Churchwardens, dashing in for a glass or two before and after every service in the Minster. But that wedding breakfast he put on for us a few years ago was quite remarkable. Everyone said so. Of course, today I'd paid Straker well over the odds but this time it was for my very own particular celebration. Mr. Welburn wouldn't have done that, God rest him. He'd never got over paying 12/6d each for tickets to a dinner to celebrate Queen Victoria's visit to Hull.

Make no mistake, I've never been one to begrudge spending money but today I found myself seized by a tremendous urge to explain this to Mrs Cussons. She's the Mayor's wife, stuffily sitting there across the table from me. Obviously, I was forced to raise my voice above the pealing of the Minster bells. Most unfortunately, people heard me screeching 'I paid for all this you know' when the chimes abruptly stopped! Quickly adopting an artful smile and in more regular tones I'd added, 'And of course I couldn't have been more delighted to do so.' Mrs. Cussons relaxed back from open mouth and raised eyebrows into the normal unremarkable state of her face, little round nose on a flat expanse of yellowy-grey skin. Like a pea on a shovel. You have to laugh.

Maybe I was quite jolly with all the wine but never what you might call 'lushy'. For hadn't I downright refused to contemplate joining the Total Abstinence Society? I like a bit of fun. My guests and I had gone down to the Hall Garth Inn after the opening of the 'Elizabeth Welburn Alms Houses' right down at the other end of Keldgate. Yes, they're actually named after me, so you can just put that in your pipe and smoke it! I'll be forever remembered in Beverley. Immortality, that's what I've achieved. Shame it was all happening after my Mr. Welburn died last year; he would have enjoyed lording it today albeit moaning about the cost of it to me later.

Mind you, that was a bit of a shock, him collapsing in front of me in the parlour. Three times that Sunday had he walked down to the Minster; always keen to stand well with heaven if only to gain advantage over his neighbours. Seemingly hale and hearty, on his return he ate a huge dinner till he must have been full as an egg. Then he grumbled about the length of the sermon and dropped dead, right there without any warning. I kept shaking him and telling him to wake up but it was no good, he'd cocked up his toes.

Apoplexy they said. I know it was a shock to me and everyone else but isn't that the best way to leave life? I wouldn't have wished him to suffer or lose his dignity; he loved his dignity. Still haven't got used to it, you know, being alone here. Just making tea for myself I'd hear his voice saying 'Ever the cup that cheers.' He always said that. Now the untidiness and ordering of my days is purely down to me, alone.

I'll tell you about the opening of my Alms Houses this afternoon. After cutting the ribbon and making a short speech I'd found a limp bouquet thrust into my hands by the daughter of some Councillor or other. I could've done with another hand to hold it and lift my skirts out of the dust while clinging on to the Mayor's sleeve to walk down the curving length of Keldgate. We led the full complement of Councillors, wives securely hooked onto their arms presenting an honest but dignified procession to any onlookers.

I've known everyone in the parade for years of course. Unlike me, they'd stayed here vegetating throughout their boring lives with never a notion of life anywhere else. But why should they bother when Beverley satisfied their every requirement? You must remember it's normal here to look down on the rest of England. Having travelled widely, I would claim to have much more understanding of the ways of the world and therefore more competence to make judgements. Well, more than any of that lot I dare say. But I have no wish to upset folk so I keep my thoughts to myself, just between you and me shall we say?

The atmosphere among the Councillors is so much easier now than in previous years because Councillor Gillyatt Sumner, their main trouble-stirrer, was absent. Don't let on, but he's still in Bradford Gaol, most likely heavily ironed. But I'll tell you more about him later. Don't know how he'll be coping with prison at his age, he's 71 you know. I do rather miss him, despite his rumoured disposition for 'infamous vices'. Our 'Beau Brummel of Beverley', spruce and self-satisfied was always good for a gossip. The rest of the council weren't fashionable like him, most had antiquity off to perfection. They probably think I'm overly ostentatious as well, but honestly why should I be ashamed of my wealth? I didn't wring it from the misery of others like some I could mention. Well not all of it anyway.

Passed Fox's grocery shop on the way along Keldgate. Of course, someone else is running it, now I've given it up. Out of habit I'd looked across at that old stone dog opposite the Brownriggs' house. I always thought it was a fox put there in honour of my Mr. Fox, even though the stone carver had given it webbed feet. Everyone who passed by made sure of their luck by giving its head a rub. Small wonder it's smooth as marble now.

The fun we used to have down that end of Keldgate when I was a girl. So many memories! As the Mayor and I walked past the corner of Lairgate, an old chap in scraggy corduroys touched his hat to me. Beside him his old dog sniffed at his boots, both dribbling. Could he be one of the lads I used to lark with?

Last week I'd traipsed down to the Hall Garth Inn to ask Mr. Straker if he would get his lads to bring up that ancient oak table from the

Court Chamber to the first-floor dining room for my special day. It could extend to over six feet when its two leaves are drawn out and had the most intricate carving you'll ever see. I'd always felt it would better suit the dining chairs he's got up there and be more in keeping with the historic celebration of my charity. Mr. Straker stroked his black curling whiskers sayng it was too heavy to shift up the stairs and besides they'd never get it through the bloody doors.

Hall Garth Inn is a rare old place, with bits of the old Manorial Court and the Debtors' Prison entangled among dingy irregular passages. The Archbishops of York had their Palace there for centuries and you'll find stone robbed from its walls all over the town. There's no natural stone round here so they don't let any go to waste.

Later on, the building reorganised itself into the Admiral Duncan Inn; you'll see his portrait still up there on the wall so everyone remembers his name. What always gets my goat is this - it's always people like Admirals, Archbishops and Provosts who get written about, but what about the debtors, the drinkers, the washerwomen and cooks and even the night soil men? They've disappeared as if they never existed but they were here and they mattered. Someone should write about what they got up to. Maybe I will, I love people's stories. Perhaps then I'll be remembered as an authoress as well as a benefactress to this town and no one will think to blame me for anything else.

But let's get back to today. As Mayor, Mr. Cussons felt he should assist me to sit at the top table. When the hefty oak chair proved too much for him, I heaved it out myself to save him the embarrassment and sat down abruptly. This acted as a signal for napkins to be flurried out and tucked in all around the room. At last, we dined.

As the rattle of cutlery gradually subsided and before conversation clamoured to previous levels, Mayor Cussons pulled himself to his feet rocking our table worryingly; another reason I'd wished for the substantial one from downstairs. He pinged on his glass with a knife for attention, fulsomely cleared his throat, before saying, 'My dear Mrs Welburn, I cannot tell you how much we appreciate your very generous gesture in providing this fine repast and of course the much-needed accommodation for three poor widows in what I may call 'stylish' new cottages at yon end of Keldgate. I'm sure everyone will agree with me that your name will be held in the highest regard in the town along with other public-spirited people such as our own Sir Michael Wharton, Mr. Christopher Eden and Mrs Margaret Ferrer.' Everyone set down their glasses and clapped their hands, some more vigorously than others I did observe.

Old Thomas Cussons waffled on in his quaint Sunderland twang, fragrance of tannery intermittently wafting from him whilst I inwardly fumed at his comparison of my charity with Margaret Ferrer's! I know for a fact that it hasn't paid out more than a few pounds every year since it started. Someone is getting the benefit but it isn't any of the deserving poor, I can tell you that. At least my poor old ladies will be living securely in solid bricks and mortar, thank you very much.

After endless speeches and raised glasses to toast 'Health and prosperity to Mrs. Welburn', the applause and cheering abruptly brought me back to the job in hand. I was off round the room, bowing and thanking, preening and protesting. Listening to the polite table chatter, clatter of cutlery and occasional laughter, I thrilled to the pleasures of benevolence. Money is a wonderful reconciler. Thankfully I was never notorious enough to be taken up by those scandalising newspapers that so tortured and taunted Princess Caroline or Lady Hamilton and Lord Nelson, poor souls. Shame he never got to see his Column.

Acting the fine gracious lady, aloof and alone, made me come over quite swimmy. Eventually, taking a last genteel turn around the room, I said my goodbyes to the lot of them with the studied decorum practised in front of my long mirror the previous night. Then began my amble back up a sunless Keldgate, bunions throbbing under a heavy sky aching to rain. Between the terraced houses I passed tiny shops selling small coal and potatoes and suchlike; of course, my own shop had catered for more refined palates with a wide range of groceries.

I still expect to see the crumbling old Bar at the far end of Keldgate; that was one of our ancient gateways into the town as you know. Layers of chalk put down to repair the road over hundreds of years had decreased the gap so much that when loaded carts could no longer get through, the Council decided to knock the whole thing down. Although I miss it, you have to admit it's very nice to see up to Westwood Common now with all the windmills turning.

Mam always insisted flour needed to rest for a month before she used it and gave me the disagreeable task of sifting out all the beetles from it. Whenever she wanted more fetching from one of the mills up there, I'd get our Bill to go with me to be on the safe side. Terrible place the Westwood was years ago; all classes would go there, putting bets on the bare knuckle fighting between the lads. It turns out it was acceptable for the son of a lord to fight a cobbler but the cobbler was liable to be arrested for striking a gentleman.

There was a chap who lodged at the Tiger Inn on North Bar Street who would take his pet bear there to be baited by dogs. Its muzzle stopped it biting so it hugged the dogs to death instead. Served them right, should have hugged the owners as well. Pa used to talk about a Mr. Hazlehurst on Beckside who made nails and such like; he bred bulldogs specially for bull-baiting. They'd stopped doing that in the middle of town the year I was born but they still do it in Newbegin Pits. If you look hard enough you can find the metal ring anchored in the ground there for tying up the poor bulls. Life is so unfair.

Now I'm back here at Albany House in all its peculiar splendour, almost next door to the new 'Elizabeth Welburn Alms Houses', I like saying that. I know some people say this place is only mine because of the death of Mr. Welburn but even before we were wed I worked hard to deposit a considerable sum into my own bank account. And today that money has been put to something laudable. This idea of providing the Alms Houses came to me after I realised that so many people I've known who are now deceased will be forever remembered by wall plaques commemorating their good works. And, I thought to myself, 'Now then, Mrs. Elizabeth Welburn, how would you wish to be remembered in Beverley?'

Inside the hallway, back pressed against my sturdy front door I kicked off those torturing shoes, skimming them over the fancy floor tiles, bringing the added benefit of cooling my feet. The remorseless ticking of the longcase clock in the hall was the only sound in the stony silence. I'll get Polly to give the floor a good scrub tomorrow and she can clean the shoes too and see if she can stretch them a bit more. I really should have gone round to her Mam's first to ask to her come and help me with this dress.

It's strange being on your own. It must be the first time in over 70 years that I have been absolutely alone with no one to speak to, rattling around like a loose nail in an empty coffin. Sadly, I'm not what is generally regarded as 'visitable' but I'll have to change all that. Quiet is singing in my ears and I can't be arsed to light the oil lamp. At some point this evening I'll have to think about how to get out of this gown Mary Hodgson fixed me up with. Perhaps I should get my own parlour maid and have her living in; a steady young woman would be best, you don't pay servant tax on them.

I'd so wanted to make a brilliant appearance among the gentlefolk of Beverley. Not wanting to dress like a duchess, merely an elegant woman of means, I'd chosen this silk satin stripe in crimson, magenta and grey. My delight in being finely dressed stems from my time in London and this gown was so lovely that when Mary brought it round, I just hung it outside the wardrobe so I could savour it. She had edged right round the back panel with a magenta silk fringe and braid; took her hours she told me. Even my shoes were to match, not that anyone saw much of them but I'd felt obliged to order them specially from Welburn's Boot and Shoe Emporium. Not being used to the heels, I'd practised round the house and then stuffed them with damp newspaper to try to stretch them to fit round my ugly red bunions. I did have such pretty feet when I was young; can't bear to contemplate them now.

In the dusk I'm afraid I used very unladylike language after nearly falling over that wretched footstool our Bill made for me years ago. When he was younger, you'd always find my brother on my father's lathe turning lengths of wood he'd scrounged to make useless bits of furniture. When his wife Amy found the stool hidden away in a cupboard, she decided to embroider a cover for it to get in my good books; she knew I didn't like her. She presented it to me with its turquoise blues and rose pinks and the most acid yellow you'd ever see. I said thank you and put it back in the cupboard.

We never got on. Happen it was her high simpering voice that put me off and her silly pretensions to being weak and helpless when in reality she was tough as Mr. Cussons' leather. I did bring the footstool to Albany House though, and showed it to Amy, proving that I'm now a much nicer person although you wouldn't have thought so when I hit my foot on it. My bunions definitely are not wanting to venture out again; I'll manage somehow to shed my stifling stays and breathe fully once more.

Shall I put my feet up on the footstool and perhaps read a book before going upstairs to take on the task of undressing? No, that would mean lighting a lamp. There's a big bookcase at the side of the fireplace. All Mr. Fox's books are still there; his nephews never wanted them. I used to run a duster over them from time to time never taking time to look at the titles. Something about lambs caught my eye. I like lambs but this is 'Lambs Tales from Shakespeare', I think Mr. Fox bought it about fifty years ago when it was published.

They put a bust of William Shakespeare above the stage at the Playhouse Theatre in Lairgate. He was very popular. A few years ago a group called the United Shakespeare Company even bought the house in Stratford where he was born just to preserve it. Mr. Fox loved his books but had to tell you about everything he read so I came to know a lot of Mr. Shakespeare's stories and, of course, I've acted in some of his plays. So long as you've a good memory you don't need to understand the words.

What a talker Mr. Fox was. He'd keep going even when no one was there in the shop to listen, muttering through that wholesome moustache of his, yellowing at the edges. I'd go off and fettle somewhere, come back and he'd still be gabbing. He wasn't just a grocer you know, he owned loads of land all round Beverley. He was on the council for donkeys' years and Mayor twice. You know he died in the Guild Hall during the 'performance of his duties'. That's how the newspapers reported it. Thank the Lord he wasn't engaged in the performance of his 'duties' with me when he dropped dead! But at least it was a quick way to go, just like my Mr. Welburn but not like my father. Mam used to say he clung to life like the old ivy stuck to the privy although the leaves had been brown and withered for years.

Deciding against reading, and up in my bedroom looking out on Keldgate, I spread my purple-veined hands against the un-shuttered window to have a good look down the road. There were stragglers reeling noisily home, swaying on and off the foot pavement, probably coming back from my do at Hall Garth Inn. Some must have put in a six-hour shift there, to my cost maybe, yet with no effect on my complacency.

I stretched my stiff fingers against the window to loosen them up. I used to have such pretty hands. Everyone said so. Long ago I did make an effort, made my own cold cream, pounded a bit of pig's lard mixed up with white wax; you had to put in a splash of rose water to get over the smell. What a waste of time. So much time wasted and now it's too late but I still like a dab of lavender water behind my ears.

Looking up the road to where Keldgate Bar used to stand, puts me in mind of all the daft childhood larks we had once we'd ventured through the archway and out on to Westwood Common. It's curious how memories emerge from nowhere. If it was just me and our Bill, we'd make it our mission to scare the crows from the skylarks' nests in the Spring and chase each other round the back of the Mill up on the highest bit of the Westwood. One day Bill found he couldn't move when his boots got stuck in the mud at the edge of the mill pond. I told him to unlace them and come out in his stocking feet. I was in trouble for a mud-stained pinny and he got a new pair of boots.

We did our patriotic duty collecting acorns in the Autumn to plant them everywhere to ensure the navy had sufficient oak for their fighting ships. Other times we'd lay in the grass at the top of a hill, arms pressed in to our sides and take it in turns to be pushed down like a barrel. Such a shame my own daughter, Harriet, never got chance to roll down those grassy slopes.

Whenever our Bill and his friend Michael Scruton with some more lads came along, their favourite game was to re-enact the Pilgrimage of Grace they'd learned about from Reverend Coltman. He often taught the boys about the history of Beverley and told them how an angry mob had gathered on the Westwood in the 16th century. Girls weren't allowed to know history.

9

I don't think any of the boys really understood what the Pilgrimage had been about but our version usually ended up with seven or eight of us doing our best to represent five hundred Beverley men who had sworn oaths there. This gave the boys an excuse to say every rude word they knew, call each other Percy and wave their sticks about. We'd all cheer at the top of our voices before setting off across the common to march to York. On the way it was the rule that everyone had to take a running jump across the Tan Gallop. The one who made it farthest then became the leader. I blame my skirts for always landing in the mud on my posterior.

On hot days the lads would find chunks of sun-dried cow turd to throw to represent cannon balls. When my pinafore got smeared with fresh cow clap, Mam always knew from the smell of damp cloth that I'd been trying to sort out my mess before she saw it. I got double the blame for trying to cover it up and for not being quick enough to dodge out of the way. Me and the lads always turned for home when we got to the knobbly old oak trees in Burton Bushes at the far end of the Westwood. No one really knew the way to York.

In those days I was always the one tagging along behind. Then for years my name was muck down this end of town, called everything from a pig to a dog because living in a street like Keldgate, everyone knows everything about you.

Obviously today, being the focus of attention for a truly worthy reason has brought me great satisfaction and has convinced me that this is the appropriate time to put things straight. Maybe I'm not that clear on dates, never having kept a journal; surely any lifetime should be measured by people and places, not by a calendar. Memories lurking silently in the dark recesses of my brain for years, I now propose to expose to the light of day. Who can tell whether getting everything off my chest will help ease my mind and relieve me of the terrible responsibility of being the only one in this world to know where the real blame lies?

Chapter 2

Which Treats of The Early Life of Miss Elizabeth Taylor

I set off all right. My mother was determined I should make a good impression on everyone. She taught me my letters before I went to school and put me in a clean pinafore first thing every morning. Mind you I wasn't so good with my arithmetic, could never get beyond counting to five. I blamed number 'six' for always reminding me of the day the tannery cat was 'sick' in our yard before expiring in agony in front of me.

Manners mattered more to Mam, 'Mind you say 'please may' to everyone' she'd say. Which I did until Mary Ann Salmond told me it sounded stupid so then I didn't. But you can be sure I always gave a smile and bob a curtsey to anyone who lived near us, especially those who lived in the big houses.

There was Mr. Farrah, he was a cabinet maker. He owned a few houses to rent out around the town so even if he wasn't selling his cabinets, he was confident of raking in a sovereign or two. That's why Mam and Pa decided to buy up cheap cottages for Pa to fix up a bit and get paying tenants in. Being property-owners, they said, was to provide for our future, mine and Bill's. My grandmother had done the same. None of the Taylor family could contemplate the shame of ever going on the Parish.

Halfway down Keldgate, Mr. Simpson lived in a large fashionable house set right next to the reeking vats of his tannery, it belongs to Mr. Cussons the Mayor now. When his men tipped the vats out into Tan Dyke at the back, no matter where you were in our house the smell caught at the back of your throat. Most people in Keldgate worked at the tanneries and most had children. We'd all play hide and seek among the tan pits but that evil smell would caused me to retch dramatically. I preferred to hide among the piles of old bark dumped down by Tan Dyke; it was fun jumping into them. Nobody ever found me; perhaps they didn't bother looking.

Our Bill got a job at the tanyard when he was older, driving the cart round, gathering up the stinking hides and relics of departed cattle. He couldn't stick at it for long so they put him on going out buying bark for the tanning. Then he came home smelling of bark, so sad at the poor horse forced to go round in circles all day to turn the bark mill; always soft was our Bill.

Mr. Fox's shop was across the road from us. I'd stick my head through the shop door just to get the treat of a sniff of fresh bread and apples even if I was just going across to the pump. Every morning I'd be sent for water, slopping it over myself when I'd filled the pail too full. Mr. Fox was 'Chamber Clerk" at the Guild Hall whatever that meant and folk said he was going to be Mayor. He was definitely the most important person I knew. I told Mary Ann Salmond that I knew someone important but she said her grandmother had been injured by an earthquake in Beverley forty years ago so she was more famous. You could never argue with her.

Down Keldgate you could always hear people coming up behind you in their hob-nailed boots or on creaky carts pulled by wheezy horses. But never my particular friend, Reverend Joseph Coltman. He would swish up silently behind you on his hobby horse then you'd hear his breath rasping out 'Good morning young lady and just what mischief have you and your Bill been up to on God's glorious morning?' He'd take my chin in one hand while holding on to his hobby horse with the other, which he said was really called a velocipede. His hands always smelt of Pears soap.

Since he was twenty-one years old he'd had to ride his hobby horse because his little legs couldn't support the weight of his great stomach. Out in the street lads shouted things like 'You didn't get that belly with fasting and praying!' Never offended, he'd just shout back, 'and not with eating and drinking either.' He was very clever; he had thousands of books and even wrote some himself. He helped me with my reading when Mam and Pa couldn't be arsed.

I liked going to school. I'd read anything I could get my hands on; tales of romantic encounters or travels to a foreign land were my particular favourites. Mam and Pa didn't begrudge paying for school, it got me from under their feet although they didn't put much store by books themselves. The Vicar said I should go to the circulating library whenever I wanted and my parents believed he knew best so obeyed him.

Don't think Mam would have understood the books I discussed with Rev. Coltman; some made me realise the horror of slavery and the unfairness of the world. Don't you think that law of nature that decrees women have to do whatever a man tells them, is also a sort of slavery? Pa said 'No daughter of mine will ever go on the stage' and Mr. Fox said, 'No servant of mine can bear a bastard child.' So what did I do? You couldn't really blame me.

But for reading books, I don't suppose I would have even known there'd been that Revolution in France. No one round here ever spoke of it although I found out later my father was all for revolting but held his peace for the sake of his business. Once I did ask Mr. Fox what he thought about such an event and he just laughed and said, 'Oh it would never happen here love. We're all too sensible even though our King George is mad as a box of frogs'. But he did tell me the truth about the Pilgrimage of Grace.

When I heard about that Mary Midgley climbing out of the dining room window at Norwood House and running off to Gretna Green in a chaise and four with Mr. William Beverley of all people, I thought 'good for you my girl, doing just what you want, never minding what others say.' My father, along with most Beverley people, was absolutely appalled because Mary was only sixteen years old. Actually Mr. Beverley's grandmother was even younger than that when she got wed.

Over the years, Mary Midgley was accepted and respected as Mrs. Beverley, so you see, people do forgive and forget eventually. Mr. Beverley's promise to eradicate 'violence and intimidation' when he became Mayor clearly didn't work out but he did become President of the Anti-Slavery Society, supporting the views of Mr. William Wilberforce and of my father. Mr. Beverley knew all about slavery because of his family owning tobacco plantations in America.

Fourteen years old was when everyone was sent out to work, some a lot younger. Our Bill had hardly been in school since he was eleven. After he knocked off going to the tannery he just went quietly working alongside Pa until he couldn't do without him.

As soon as I was 14, without warning, Mam said, 'Now then our Lizzie, Mr. Fox has agreed to take you on to work in the shop. First thing tomorrow morning you get yourself across there. Make sure you scrub your hands and do just what he tells you.'

I was mortified, 'Aw Mam, I don't want to work in a shop, I'd hate it.'

'Listen to me Miss, it's not down to you. Your life is down to me and your father. Nothing's down to you, do you hear me?' and Mam gave me a shove into the scullery to make her point. Mother and father had owned a grocery shop before I was born and my uncle had a large one in Saturday Market; his son is running it now. No one had ever said much in favour of shop keeping, calling it a hand to mouth existence. So why would it cross my mind that I was destined for work in a grocer's shop?

Lacking other options, I went along with it. At least I wasn't forever doing laundry, getting my hands all red and sore; Mr. Fox had a washerwoman for that. But, looking back, it was from that day when I crossed the street and began working for him that I said farewell forever to the careless freedom of childhood. From not caring about rolling around on the Westwood, distributing dirt about my person, I now had to scrub my nails and appear kempt.

There was also a change in the political atmosphere. My Pa being of a Radical frame of mind, was in favour of improving life for the masses whereas, Mr. Fox had quite a different view of the world. He said 'The upper classes are born to rule, it was what they have been educated to do. What would your tannery worker know about running the business?'

I can see both sides, particularly after living in London. There you can see how money trickles down from the rich, providing opportunities for parvenus like me who possess the wit are able to seize any chance to improve their finances and their standing in society.

The worst aspect of my new life was Alice Hardaker, Mr. Fox's housekeeper. She had a heart the texture of old wood, worm-eaten with bitterness. From the start she'd decided to hate me, always trying to get me into bother with Mr. Fox for she knew that would upset me greatly.

As Mam hadn't succeeded in schooling me in the arts of housekeeping, I found tending the shop more agreeable. Arranging goods, chatting to customers, dealing with the money and a bit of light dusting suited me. And Mr. Fox came to realise I was far better for his business than Mrs. Hardaker who had a nasty habit of accusing regular customers of stealing, being particularly ill-disposed to children. Mary Ann Salmond told me that Mrs. H. had once dropped a bottle into her basket and demanded payment for it if she didn't wish Mr. Fox to be informed. I was so much more welcoming to customers; people liked me then. And it didn't take long for me to realise that it was preferable to greet them with 'how nice to see you' rather than 'how are you' thus avoiding a rigmarole of aches and worries.

Mr. Fox, so unlike my father, never stopped talking. He would transfix you with his pale blue eyes drawing you in to whatever it was he wished to impart. Descriptions of every mundane hour held your attention; no opportunity was granted for interjection. He could recall the names and foibles of every one of his customers. However whenever one tried to express their own opinions he would listen to half of their sentence, interrupting to elaborate and then explain it back to them, thus making it his own property. With convincing sincerity, he assured his customers he had kept certain goods back especially for them, for he knew only they would have the intelligence to appreciate their quality and scarcity.

Not only did he know what was unquestionably best for his customers but also for me. Unwittingly I was directed in my choice of clothes, hairstyle, way of speaking, even my way of thinking. I just had to obey him and all would be well. Mam sometimes asked why I never worked things out for myself rather than relying on Mr. Fox's opinions; I was a mere parrot, repeating words I'd been taught. My life became much easier once I learned to accept that Mr. Fox always knew best.

Chapter 3

Miss Hannah Murphy is Esteemed as an Actress

Was I happy working for Mr. Fox? It's hard to say. Because I came to relish his praise, I strove to earn it by doing everything he wished. On the other hand, because I was expected to hand my wage directly over to Mam, I grew fed up with working long hours yet never having a sixpence to scratch myself.

Having resigned myself to being forever at the beck and call of family and Fox my life abruptly changed when Mr. Ambrose Peacock built a new theatre. It stood in all its glory in Lairgate, just around the corner from our house. Everyone had wondered at the amount of land he'd been buying up but he proved his perspicacity with the immediate success of his theatre. Even the lane next to it became known as Playhouse Lane. Every new play brought playgoers of all ranks with tickets to occupy the six hundred seats available. They arrived in coaches, carriages, even sedan chairs but most jostled along on foot.

Everything changed! With my vast theatrical experience behind me, I now feel confident to justify my decisions by quoting from 'Julius Caesar', 'There is a tide in the affairs of men (or women of course) when taken at the flood lead on to fortune. Omitted, all the voyage of their life is bound in shallows and in miseries.' I did actually hear this declaimed by Mr. Edmund Keane playing Brutus at Drury Lane Theatre. However, at twenty years of age, I was merely a woman subject to impulse, harbouring an audacious wish to become mistress of my own destiny.

Whenever a new theatre company arrived in Lairgate I made it my business to go snooping round to see what was going on, reading the playbills and trying to get a glimpse of the actors. One June day a coach pulled up and the driver began unloading scores of baskets and bags, piling them beside the gault brick Playhouse walls. A lad opened the door and there was I, quick as Jimmy Roberts, picking up a huge bag and carrying it through into the musty, dank passageway. And, I swear to you, this was the very first time I'd ventured into a theatre.

I coughed apologetically previous to yelling 'Where do want this then?'

'Oh just pitch it in there will you? That one's Miss Murphy's,' said the lad, head lowered over a ledger and without a glance at me, pointed to a door.

He must have been referring to a particularly elegant woman I'd observed getting out of a carriage. She looked famous. So, arms clasped around the bag, I backed into the door, pushing it open with my posterior before almost falling over that very lady's feet. She just laughed at me and told me which other bags were hers and where to put everything. She was really friendly saying, 'I haven't seen you before my dear, are you new?'

'Mr. Butler said I should make myself useful,' said I, hastily recalling a name from the playbill.

'Did he indeed? Well, my dear, hang those few gowns up over there and tidy round in here and then you may come and watch us trying out on the stage, you'll find it interesting, I'm sure.' Miss Murphy had an engaging way with her, seeming genuinely pleased to have some company.

I found I had the words perfectly after hearing them only twice, but she seemed to have so much trouble, screwing up her eyes, shaking her head and muttering to herself. When we returned to the dressing room, she got me to tell her the lines for her to repeat over and again. I don't believe she read as well as me.

From that day I turned up at the theatre daily after the shop closed to help her dress for the performance and to arrange her hair; Miss Murphy's was a lot like mine – thick and pale gold. Mother always got me to put her hair up so I was used to it. Alice Hardaker complained about me even more when she saw me rushing my work to get finished and interrogated me as to why I was in such a chase. I never let on of course. Luckily for me Mr. Fox chose to close his doors earlier than other grocers, taking the view if folk hadn't got what they wanted by half past four then it was their look out. I told Mam I was helping do the bookkeeping.

Going through that door into the theatre absolutely changed my life, it was so different from the humdrum pace of the shop. Actors will say anything that comes into their heads without fear or favour. That Edmund Keane, he could go from lively to severe in a breath. Well powdered and as corky as you like especially after a glass or two, he would run his hand through his curls to tumble them round his face thinking to look like a cherub. He actually looking a complete coxcomb in his apple green coat with steel buttons big as crown pieces. Hearing a remark that reminded him about anything or anyone would send Mr. Keane off, delivering one of his great long speeches. Alcohol had no effect on his memory. From my initial entrancement, after two weeks he became dreadfully wearisome to me. His on-stage performance as Macbeth disappointed because he would look out for handsome women in the audience to give them a nod or a wink over the footlights. Would a great actor do that?

My first night in the pit stands out in my memory still. Waiting for the curtain to be drawn, my heartbeat quickened with the smell of the whale oil lamps ranged across the front of the stage and the rising prattle of the audience. I sat near the back straining to hear Hannah Murphy as Lady Macbeth declare 'All the perfumes of Arabia will never sweeten this little hand.' Her words sent shivers down my spine but had no effect on the groups of soulless men yarning at the back.

The weeks spent with the company positively flew by; I loved every moment with them. When the time came to help with the packing ready for the move to the next town, my spirits had fallen to their lowest until Miss Hannah Murphy said to me, 'Elizabeth my darling girl, I would absolutely adore it if you came along with me on the tour. I declare I cannot contemplate managing without you now.'

I darted a look at her wondering, was she mocking or serious? But no, she looked truly anxious, 'We must be ready for the coach early tomorrow morning you know so I beg you to decide quickly. Please,

please do come. You would get a wage and board and lots of amusement I promise you.' I assure you actual tears welled in her eyes! Perhaps our particular attachment stemmed from us actually looking quite alike; several had taken us for sisters.

Straggling back home I turned things over in my head and pingled so over my tea that Mam thought I was ill. In fact, as she appeared so concerned, I almost decided to stay but, in my heart I knew I could never be satisfied with the life in which I'd been placed. Whether my parents would have tried to stop me or not, I have no idea. I reasoned, just as everyone had forgiven Mary Midgley and William Beverley, eventually they would get over me absconding. Bill had always been their favourite child so perhaps my absence could make them love me a little bit more.

That evening I packed a bag with as much as I could easily carry before writing a note for Mam and my father, saying goodbye and requesting them to let Mr. Fox know I had left his employment and for them to collect my wages. After a night of fitful sleep, I slunk silently through the kitchen door and into the misty grey-green morning. I still can recall that damp, dewy smell of the road as I left the only home I'd ever known.

 Maybe Mam wouldn't have chowed at me for wanting to be in the theatre but I couldn't take the chance of her forbidding me. Although she was no Quaker, never would she think of entering a playhouse herself. She did know I was unhappy drudging for Mr. Fox in his shop; I was always moaning about that bitch Alice Hardaker making my life such a misery, pushing and pinching me. Only the other day she'd deliberately spilt milk over the front step after I'd scrubbed it; I certainly wouldn't miss her.

Life had generally been very pleasant when I was that carefree little girl running round Keldgate. I was Jack Taylor's bonny little lass and Billy Taylor's annoying sister. Jack Taylor was a builder and joiner. I know I used to think 'Why wasn't he called Jack Builder'? If he'd actually been a tailor, I could have helped him, picking up pins and writing down measurements. I was no use as a builder's apprentice but our Bill was, strong in the arm and soft in the head. Bacon-brain I called him. He didn't like me mocking him because he couldn't read very well and I could.

That bit of Shakespeare keeps going round in my head whenever I think of Bill - 'He that has a little tiny wit, With heigh ho, the wind and the rain, Must make content with his fortunes fit, though the rain it raineth every day.' Edmund Keane used to sing it.

I'm ashamed to say my jealousy of Bill caused me to try to get him into trouble when we were small. One summer I convinced him that everyone in Beverley considered it good luck to run across Keldgate and back twelve times to touch the stone dog while the Minster clock was striking noon. The last time he did it, Bill was on his final dash as Pa came out of the house and grabbed him just before he went under a cart. Bill got skelped and so did I. I didn't cry but I can still see my big brother, huge tears making white stripes down his grubby cheeks, blubbing that I'd told him to do it.

I protested that the true blame should belong to Pa as I'd overheard him laughing with Mam about One-armed Harry who drank twelve pints of ale in the Spotted Cow in Wednesday Market while the Minster clock struck twelve. All the customers paid for his beer and cheered him on. He was a local hero. Unjustly my parents refused to believe my assertion that my only intention was to make our Bill a local hero too. I became the scapegoat as usual.

So perhaps our Bill would miss me because I wouldn't be there to be blamed for everything. If he wet himself it was only because I'd made him laugh. If he broke a window with his ball, I should have caught it. He was the lad, to be indentured for the joinery business like my father in spite of him stammering like a jelly. No, I concluded, there were more reasons to leave than to stay.

So that morning, off I went to where the theatre company were waiting on Lairgate. Without a backward look, I boarded the coach determined never to repent my decision. I'd never really been further than Walkington before and that was only two miles away so my stomach took a long time to get used to the interminable rattling and shaking of the carriage.

The seasoned travelling actors had so much to tell me. Take food with you, they advised, for even if you'd paid for a meal at an inn, it didn't mean you had the time to eat it and the landlady wouldn't be bothered too much because she would just sell it again to the next coach arriving. And, they said, if the horses took off at a gallop, you should hold tight to your bench and never ever try to leap out. They also warned about how expensive it could be if you didn't watch out. All the people at staging posts wanted tipping and would overcharge for candles and food and so forth.

Theatre people were always in such a ferment of neediness. Whether it was food, drink, or reassurance I was there for them. I blended their rouge with gum Arabic so it lasted longer. I fetched and carried, dressed, combed and listened. Oh my word, how I listened. Actors just love to be listened to and I treated all the same. But then, there I was in another exciting World, a new person with a past just waiting for me to invent.

My way of preparing tooth powder for the company proved to be exceedingly popular. Much cheaper than Mrs. Trotters' which sold at 2/9d a box in London, I made a concoction of baking powder and soap with a dash of peppermint to freshen the breath just as Mr. Fox had taught me. The actors would all bring me their little pots to fill and slip me a few coins. The women in the company were particularly determined not to have to resort to walrus ivory or porcelain teeth and recoiled at the thought of what they now call 'Waterloo teeth' which are real teeth gathered from the dead on the battlefields or from poor children.

We went to lots of towns; I saw so many inns and theatres you would not believe it. Comedies like 'Wild Oats and 'No Song for Supper' always went down well and you know how actors like a good joke. So even the long hours of coach travel passed quickly with all the story-telling and laughter. The company varied as we travelled. Managers changed, people got sick or decided to settle down somewhere that pleased them. Mostly I stuck close to my mentor Miss Murphy, the nationally acclaimed actress.

Blue devils molested Miss Hannah quite often. She became badly affected by a distressing experience in a certain town when the audience began mooing at her after she'd stumbled over her lines several times. I'd sit on her daybed, stroking her arm and trying to jolly her out of her fears when she was desponding. By the time we got down to London I'd decided on a scheme which would suit us both. From now on I would encourage her to give everything up and go home to her ageing mother and I would take her place in the company! How selfless is that?

Her weakened temperament made it easy to persuade her into my way of thinking. 'It must be so frightening for you to stand out on that stage in front of thousands of people, all waiting for you to forget your lines,' I'd say encouragingly.

'Yes, yes my tongue actually sticks to the very roof of my mouth with such terror, I can barely speak,' she agreed.

'Just think, the Drury Lane Theatre holds almost 4,000 people! That's about half the population of my home town, quite astonishing don't you think?' I'd laugh casually. Miss Murphy confessed her heart always started going like the clappers at such a thought; tears moistened her cheeks at the drop of a hat.

'Oh, how I miss my own mother and if she were ill I'd be dashing back to Beverley I can assure you of that' I told her consolingly, dabbing my own eyes. Eventually she decided for herself that she could no longer continue to perform and I sunned myself in the delight of that very moment when we embraced and said our fond goodbyes.

Miss Murphy's greatest concern had been that she'd promised to fulfil her run at Drury Lane Theatre and was reluctant to let anyone down but there again she was unhappy beyond measure. Out of the kindness of my heart, hadn't I offered to fulfil her contract myself? Why should she demur? After all I knew her lines and moves. Her clothes fitted me and we had the same colouring and similar features. You may think I was taking advantage of her easily moulded temperament or, you may think I was taking a huge risk venturing to adopt her perilous life. In those days I was fearless. How could anything possibly go wrong?

Although the few remaining members of the company realised what we'd done, they thought it quite amusing and went along with the subterfuge as I'd looked after them all so well while we were travelling together. I worked hard at replicating Hannah's constantly sweet face but so long as the performances went on and the company and I got paid, everything was exactly as anyone could wish.   The actors mostly thought kindly of me, seeing that I remembered my lines and movements more accurately than Hannah ever did.   Actually, Edmund Keane was the only one still there who had come all the way down from Yorkshire with Hannah and me but being always in his cups, he could never recall anyone's name anyway

You may expect appearing at the famous Drury Lane Theatre to be beyond all the reasonable expectations of a naïve girl from a small town. But I took everything in my stride; straight away I understood London to be the perfect place for me.   Every evening the theatre shimmered with dazzling turbans and Prince of Wales feathers. Many ladies wore those Frenchified muslin dresses with high waists and narrow skirts, wantonly baring their arms and feet; obviously it was a lot warmer in London than draughty old Beverley. You'd find the more sedate ladies keeping to their silk petticoats and long bodices but, in those days, no one really wanted to dress like aristocrats, not after what had happened to them in France but a few decades before.

Drury Lane Theatre owed its style and beauty to a very famous architect named Mr. Robert Adam Hannah informed me; she should have designed buildings herself for she loved architecture so much.   She knew all the styles, Baroque, Palladian and whatnot. Mr. Adam had insisted on swags of plaster flowers arranged round the balconies. The theatre was five galleries high and the plasterwork on the ceiling was so enormous your poor neck ached before you saw the full size of it. Anyone up in the Gods needed opera glasses for viewing the stage. A press room below the stage housed printers printing everything - playbills, prompt books and tickets in every type face imaginable.

Of course, all this was before it burned down.

Chapter 4

Melodrama

On being introduced to Mr. Richard Sheridan the owner of Drury Lane Theatre I ventured to ask whether he was familiar with my home town of Beverley. I knew he'd written a play entitled 'A Trip to Scarborough' which of course is also in Yorkshire. Unfortunately, he wished to discuss another play written by someone named Molière. When in all innocence I enquired 'Molly who?' he hastily excused himself and rushed away on some urgent theatre business. I found no other opportunity to ask whether he had encountered characters like his Sir Tunbelly Clumsey or Lord Foppington in Beverley or even in Scarborough. I now blush to recall that first encounter.

I wrote to Reverend Coltman asking him to give Mam and Pa my address as Drury Lane Theatre, London and to tell them of my meeting with Richard Sheridan, the great playwright. His name meant nothing to them of course.

After my first few minutes of appearing on stage, I felt completely at my ease. Heckling held no worries for me as it had for Hannah. All my life I'd experienced chiding and jeering so why would a noisy London audience bring me to tears? My strategy was to keep my eyes glancing around the galleries; you couldn't really see into the boxes and you just had to ignore the pit. The chief ambition of all actors was to be heard above the hubbub of that surging mass down in the pit - eating, drinking and accosting the trollops blatantly plying their trade in order to recoup the shilling they'd paid for their ticket.

The effusions of praise and lewd comments I attracted when recognised out in the streets was something I learned to cope with. On the stage I'm happy to relate that I was never mooed at or pelted with food although those in the orchestra were sometimes hit when missiles fell short.

One member of the Drury Lane Company I got to know really well was Michael Macready who acted a bit, shifted scenery, posted up play bills or whatever the manager wanted him to do. There was a whim and humour in him that I really liked. The way he would look, one eyebrow quizzically raised, before bursting into laughter at my wonderment at the grandeur of London quite endeared him to me. My careless remark about how the bright stuccoed walls of the buildings quite dazzled me after being used to the dull brick of Beverley caused him great hilarity.

Michael spoke nonsense delightfully. He was full of mischievous anecdotes of the Green Room and the many actors he'd known. My mother would have complained about the way his hair hung long and untidy to his shoulders and how his neck cloth contrived always to be hanging loose at his throat as if he was too busy to tie it securely. I found it stylish.

Michael was a real Cockney born and bred even with such a Scottish sounding name. He was so proud of all the new mansions going up and desperate keen to show London off to me. I would select one of Hannah's fashionable gowns she'd left behind, usually my favourite with body and sleeves of black velvet bound with pink ribbon and a pink petticoat. Michael cut a dash in his blue coat and shabby velvet breeches as we joined the rest of the 'beau monde.'

In select Chocolate Houses like Ozinda's we'd catch up on the news and listen in to gallant conversation that we'd later imitate and mock. I usually had to slip Michael the coins to pay the bill as he was always pleading being 'a bit dammed low in the water' meaning he'd been gambling. Then we'd hurry off back to Drury Lane to prepare for the next performance.

Pacing side by side round the streets whenever not required at the Theatre there was delight to be found in being part of what Michael called the 'procession of human improvement'. Every corner offered vistas of elegant houses set around green spaces tidily incorporated into squares and parks. In contrast Beverley has wide acres of unkempt common land encircling the town of smoke-stained, cramped houses; their gardens lie confined unseen behind high brick walls.

A stroll along Pall Mall was one of my favourite outings. I remember going there one June day when they were putting up gas lamps specially to celebrate mad King George's birthday. We joked that this innovation could send him into further confusion if he thought the stars had suddenly fallen from the sky. I know we have gas lights in Beverley now but Pall Mall lit the way so to speak.

Michael showed me the charming house where Nell Gwyn had once lived. 'How profitable it is to be a king's whore,' he said. And there was Carlton House, a vast, alternative palace used when the Prince fell out with his father. This was where, according to scandal-mongers, all kinds of intemperance took place. Mrs. Fitzherbert lived there for a time until the Prince Regent was pressured to marry his cousin Caroline. 'One damned German Frau is as good as another' he said. After treating her like dirt he kept going back to Mrs. Fitzherbert, who of course claimed to be his lawful wedded wife.

When Miss Jane Austen wrote of Queen Caroline, 'poor woman, I shall support her as long as I can because she is a woman and because I hate her husband.' Everyone agreed for when, after becoming King George IV, he died, the Times newspaper printed, 'There never was an individual less regretted by his fellow creatures'. But there's one thing you can say about him, he did love his architecture and although Buckingham House was never his home, all the remodelling he'd ordered has eventually benefited our blessed Queen Victoria and her family hasn't it? After the demolition of the extravagant Pall Mall 'Palace' it was gratifying to see its elegant columns thriftily re-erected outside the National Gallery.

For the first time in my life, I walked over water when Michael took me along the wooden bridge at Putney to actually cross the River Thames. I gripped the rail tightly with both hands, unsettled by the view of the moving water below and clouds unfurling above. In order to conceal my giddiness, I mooted what I thought was a particularly sagacious question, 'What I wish to know Michael, is why we say 'Tems' when we mean this river. Should we not pronounce it with the 'th' as it is written?'

Michael as usual was delighted to demonstrate his vast local knowledge. 'I fear we must put the blame for that anomaly purely on our first King George who came here having no English whatsoever; he couldn't even make a speech at the State Opening of Parliament. As it was impossible for him to pronounce 'th' of Thames, to humour him, all his courtiers said 'Tames' which eventually degenerated into 'Tems'. It's as simple as that.'

'Why write it down with an aitch then? How nonsensical,' said I.

'Oh no one in London puts much store on spelling don't you know. There's not many here can read so we just make the best of what we hear. We say Elephant and Castle instead of 'La Infanta de Castile' so now we're stuck with the River Tems.' Michael spoke with such authority, back then I never found reason to query anything he said.

On another day we walked alongside the new docks built in the marshland beside the Thames passing the murky cottages of the dock workers. He pointed out the stark contrast between them and those large houses of the merchants and shipowners whose staithes led down to the riverside where eyes could be kept on businesses. Ships from all over the world anchored there to be fitted out. Some were being prepared to carry the thousands of soldiers to the Cape of Good Hope to save it from Napoleon's hankering to rule the whole world.

Wandering far and wide with Michael, I became more confident of my bearings, knowing I could always find my way back to Drury Lane Theatre by watching out for the massive statue of Apollo on the roof. Easy enough in broad daylight but by late afternoon when the smoke from all the chimneys of years past descended onto the streets, nothing much could be seen through the fogs.

One Wednesday we'd been to the Natural History Specimen Collection in Piccadilly to see sixty species of stuffed monkey before carrying on to Covent Garden Market which, Michael informed me, was formerly a 'Convent Garden' belonging to Westminster Abbey.

Now a bustling area, it is occupied by women 'portresses' dressed almost like men, smoking and drinking gin. Their muscular necks were as wide as their heads from the heavy baskets of market produce lifted on to their heads for delivery around the city.

Michael insisted I tore myself away from staring at these Amazons as this outing was specially planned for me to visit Covent Garden Theatre to meet the magnificent Mrs Sarah Siddons in her private dressing room no less! Her brother, Mr. John Kemble, had persuaded her to play Lady Macbeth in his spectacular new production. It was the talk of the town.

Michael said, 'You will absolutely adore her, she is the most brilliant actress you'll ever see and so beautiful, everyone says Shakespeare himself must lean out of heaven to watch her.'

He led me through the stage door along a gloomy, dusty corridor until we were confronted by a maid feverishly pushing a cloud of wayward curls away from her eyes. Her face lit up with pleasure as she recognised Michael. 'Go in, go in, Mr. Macready, Madam will be delighted to see you. You know how tedious she finds it waiting for curtain call.' Michael gave her a wink and whispered in my ear as we went further into the building, 'She's one of the dollymops here. The actors all adore her.'

Never having heard the term before, I stood in ignorant silence as Michael gave a ripple rap on the half-open door. Pulling me round he arranged our two heads to poke around the dressing room door together to greet the famous lady. He was quite correct. No one could exaggerate the beauty of Sarah Siddons' full lips and dark eyes. I was completely captivated. Michael quietly introduced me as Miss Hannah Murphy and she dashed me a dazzling smile while her hand was proffered for a kiss from Michael. Her plain red morning dress, frilled round the neck disclosing a discreet gold necklet, suited her immensely.

'How lovely it is to have visitors!' she said, inviting us to find somewhere to sit with a dramatic double wave of the hand. 'We'll have a dish of tea I think,' reaching out to quiver a bell. Turning to me she said 'And how is Drury Lane nowadays?' Then dropped her voice to inquire, 'Do tell me my dear, have you met the ghost?'

'You have said nothing of a ghost Michael,' I squealed, hand to throat, feigning alarm in a predictably theatrical manner.

'I assure you I've never encountered him myself. Apparently, he's a harmless old man dressed in grey with a tricorn hat and a sword he keeps sheathed; he's been there for some time. All theatres do have their special ghost you know.' He stroked my knee comfortingly.

'For myself, I would never like to be alone there. Such a wilderness of a place don't you find?' said Mrs. Siddons tilting her head to slyly wink at me.

In my innocence I said 'Oh have you been there, Mrs. Siddons?' How she laughed at that, 'Only for about twenty years was it not Michael? I played a few roles there when I was just starting out. It must be said that I wasn't well received. Shamefully banished as a worthless candidate for fame and fortune but, eventually, I succeeded in getting over that first little setback.'

Her lively face changed dramatically from a picture of regret to glowing stoically with heroic determination. I'm sure she could sense I was embarrassed by my ignorance for straight away she said 'And where are you from my dear? Not a cockney sparrow, I detect from your voice.'

And there was me thinking I'd rid myself completely rid of my Yorkshire vowels but I made light of it. 'No Mrs Siddons, you surmise correctly, I'm from a place in the north of England called Beverley. You've probably never heard of it.'

'I certainly have my dear,' she beamed at me, 'And I'm sure I've played in a sweet theatre there once when I was on the York circuit. Such a dear little town I do recall.' Her maid came in with a tray of tea things and set it down on the table beside me so I took it upon myself to pour, trying to steady my unsteady hands.

But Sarah Siddons' voice! So mesmerising, I declare I could have listened to her forever, perhaps it was the Welsh lilt. She told me about some of the productions she had been involved in. In one play, she described how engineers had contrived to have gallons of water actually gushing down rocks into a lake on the stage. Her story of the time when our King George was shot at when he was attending Drury Lane Theatre left me gasping. I don't think such news had ever reached Beverley.

'Oh yes my dear, I was there. I actually heard the report,' she assured me.

'But who would do such a thing? The man must have been lost to all his senses,' said I, totally shocked.

Languorously lounging back on her day bed, Mrs. Siddons told me the story. 'Well, it was this strange young man named James Hadfield. Apparently, after sustaining a huge cut to the head when he'd been fighting in France terrible delusions began to get inside his brain. One of his weird beliefs was that if he could get himself executed for murdering the king then that would bring about the Second Coming of Christ. You must recall the upset it caused, Michael?'

'Not really, I must have been out of London at that time', said Michael.

'I suppose it was eight or nine years ago now and this Mr. Hadfield did not get his wish to be hung. He became a Bedlamite instead; he devoutly believed his own mythology. But what a terrible shot he was when you consider his military training. Totally missed the King even though he was a sitting duck, ensconced up there in the Royal Box under his red velvet canopy. I was backstage but I could hear the orchestra playing the National Anthem when suddenly, two deafening shots rang out. The echo went right round the building. The whole place was in an absolute uproar I can assure you. But do you know, it was the King himself who insisted that the show should carry on, God bless him,' Mrs. Siddons laughed.

'No one else would understand the workings of a fevered mind as well as our King, I'm sure,' muttered Michael.

Mrs. Siddons ignored this uncharitable aside. Her smile incised creases in her white face powder as she praised her monarch's bravery but then sniggered as she recalled being so startled by the loud bang, she'd lost her grip on the chamber pot clenched between her thighs and no one noticed the mess backstage as all were rushing around in a frenzy.

Glancing at my shocked face she added as she winked knowingly, 'After all my dear it's not what you actually do that matters, it's what people see you do. You should always remember that.' And I certainly have. Mrs. Siddons did beg us to come back to see her again and I so wanted to but alas that never happened.

Sharing bread, cheese and beer after a performance of the 'Prisoner at Large,' Michael and I discussed what Mrs Siddons had told us and off we went to explore the Royal Box, carrying lit candles. Jubilantly we discovered the actual hole made by James Hadfield's bullet. Unfortunately the floor had been swept clean of sovereigns.

Chapter 5

An Account of The Duel between Mr. George Canning and Lord Castlereagh

For several weeks following my meeting with Mrs. Siddons I privately applied myself to bringing my vowel sounds closer to hers. With her intonation even a reference to chamber pots held not a single essence of vulgarity. I trained myself to enter a room as I imagined she would, as though my presence should be regarded as the highest compliment I could possibly pay to those assembled there.

One particular evening stands out in my mind from my time at Drury Lane. I'd risked peeping through a gap in the curtain to ascertain the reason for the extraordinarily loud clangour issuing from the audience. All heads had turned toward a tall gentleman in a dark green figured-velvet jacket with complicated buttons. His chin, held so unnaturally high by his exorbitantly tall collar, would have enabled a first-class view into the nostrils of a taller man, had he so wished.

I later discovered this dandy was Lord Castlereagh, the Secretary for War. His suicide, committed years later was due, so they say, to the rumour about him 'preferring men'. To be fair to the noble gentleman, he did say he thought the person he'd propositioned was a woman. Doubt about the matter existed or he would have surely been hanged.

Whether people hated Lord Castlereagh for being a molly or for being born an aristocrat with all the excesses of privilege, it is impossible to determine. Could he help being the Marquess of Londonderry or being attracted to other men? I don't believe so, just as I couldn't help being Elizabeth Taylor. Singularly as I had voluntarily chosen to become Hannah Murphy, I felt myself driven to become more impressive than the real one. In addition to my frenzied whirl of acquiring the accomplishments required by the bon ton, I rehearsed and explored London with Michael. My primary concern however was to constantly deliver rapturously received performances at the theatre.

To be fully accepted as the leading lady, like Mrs. Siddons I wore floating draperies, exposed my arms and shoulders and adopted a particular air of boldness which seemed to go down well within the company. As well as many gowns, Miss Hannah Murphy also bequeathed to me some of her sparkling jewellery and a most sumptuous ermine muff, conscious such fripperies would be entirely out of place in her mother's cottage. Only too anxious to oblige, I made them my own. These were halcyon days.

One autumnal afternoon Michael Macready announced he wished me to accompany him to meet a gentleman named George Canning. A light breeze blew crisped leaves along the paths as we sat on a seat just inside Hyde Park; I was glad I'd brought my muff. We tarried there just long enough for Michael to enlighten me about the man we were about to meet. It turned out that not only was he Michael's half-brother, but also the Foreign Secretary in the Government. I knew little about London politics but, clearly, he was a man of some import.

Strolling near the lake, we came across Mr. Canning stiffly sitting on a bench, hands planted on his knees as the wind rummaged his sandy hair. Immediately after pleasantries were concluded, Michael asked 'Now George I have the feeling something serious must have occurred for you to wish to see me at such short notice.'

As Mr. Canning turned his long nose doubtfully across to me and back at Michael, he understood he was dumbly being asked whether I was trustworthy. 'Miss Murphy is the acme of confidentiality, I will absolutely guarantee her discretion no matter what you are about to say,' he assured his brother.

Immediately Mr. Canning came out with his dilemma, his voice pitched a tone higher than previously, he rapidly blurted, 'Lord Castlereagh has challenged me to a duel. A duel, can you believe it? In my whole life I've never even held a gun!' He was shaking his head while looking down at the slight quivering in his hands.

'Slow down sir, something must have happened between you to upset him so', said Michael.

'Sorry Michael. It seems our differences emerged after I'd been pointing out to the House that as Secretary for War, Castlereagh was responsible for risking the lives of our soldiers in Corunna. He immediately jumped to his feet and told me to mind my own business. Previously there was never a hint of ill feeling between us.' Mr. Canning shook his head. I know this will be hard for you to believe as most newspapers later described the two gentlemen as being arch rivals for years.

'Perhaps he misunderstood you, Sir. Surely that wouldn't have led to him challenging you to a duel,' I put in placatingly.

Mr. C. glanced at me, 'Well, in actual fact you are correct, I did say a few more things. As Foreign Secretary you must understand it incumbent upon me to inform the whole House that it was entirely the Secretary for War's fault that our army had to fight for their lives after finding not one single ship organised to bring them home; consequently, we lost the whole of North Spain to the French. I had a lot of support from the House for that disclosure. But did his Lordship show any sign of contrition? No, not a glimmer and so, quite reasonably you must agree, I did demand his dismissal. The only other thing I can do is to resign myself.'

Some say it was Mr. Canning himself who'd insisted on the duel which I cannot believe to be the case for that day in Hyde Park he was undeniably panic-stricken. In an effort to calm the wretched man down I said 'Oh sir, surely it will soon blow over for Lord Castlereagh will have no wish to receive even more vilification from the newspapers.'

Michael also tried to dissuade his half-brother from rash action, 'George, just reflect. Why would you give up such a remunerative appointment when there really is no need? Accept his challenge! Everyone knows Members of Parliament can't be prosecuted for murder or even for manslaughter.'

That produced a wry smile from Mr. Canning, 'Why should that matter to me? How is it a consolation to know that once I've been shot dead, he'd get off Scot free?' After further conversation Mr. Canning made the decision to accept the challenge, hoping to call Lord Castlereagh's bluff and trust he would back down. At least our Hyde Park meeting enabled him to air his problems and gather his thoughts together sufficiently to explain them rationally to his wife.

His mind seemingly settled, Mr. C. abruptly re-presented himself as a courteous gentleman full of knowledge about the history of the capital city and its people, although he insisted he was an Irishman at heart, merely born in London. It was very pleasant there, in the Park well away from the bustle and smell of the streets. Leaves were just turning colour and trickling to the grass. A swoop of swallows gathering in preparation to fly away, unexpectedly brought a lump to my throat as I visualised the same thing simultaneously occurring among the trees up on Westwood Common.

My desire to learn more about the city was gratified by Mr. Canning telling me about the Serpentine lake, created at great expense by damming up the River Westbourne for purely picturesque reasons. He also pointed out the place where Mr. Oliver Cromwell once fell from his coach and was dragged along when his feet caught in the harness.

'Hyde Park is not always this peaceful you know Miss Murphy. It's hard to believe but at certain times of the day you could come across several knights of the realm with drawn pistols, bent on defending their life and honour,' he smiled ruefully. 'My problem is not an uncommon one.'

'That's true you know,' agreed Michael, 'our revered Mr. Sheridan told me when he'd challenged a fellow forty years ago, they'd found Hyde Park so crowded the whole party had to clear off and find some quieter place to do their duelling. Of course, back then they needed a bit more space for dodging about with swords. Poor old Sherry actually ended up with a blade through his ear. Next time you speak to him make sure you get up close enough to see through the hole!'

'Fiery chap, Sheridan. He has Irish connections like me, you know, but a damned Whig of course,' said Mr. Canning, consulting his pocket watch and bowing himself away with what my mother would have called 'gracious condensation'

Only a few days after our Hyde Park meeting, Michael received yet another note from Mr. Canning pleading for his help after receiving the letter from Lord Castlereagh demanding 'satisfaction from you to which I feel myself entitled to lay claim.' George Canning calmly accepted the challenge and arrangements were made for the very next day. Another of his half-brothers, Aubrey had told him his duty was to commit to the duel in order to defend the honour of the family. Michael had scoffed, 'What honour?'

You see, honour is what aristocrats understand, they have no compunction about killing each other for a principle. Perhaps Lord Castlereagh would actually have preferred to die by someone else's hand than be driven to kill himself later.

Both Mr. Canning and Lord Castlereagh honourably resigned from the Government, leaving them vulnerable to prosecution for duelling; it would be impossible to keep such an affair a secret. They both kept away from of Parliament for some time afterwards and King George was obliged to persuade Mr. Spencer Percival to form a government. Years later Mr. Canning was in the news once more for threatening to resign from the Government, this time in support of Queen Caroline, leading to speculation that he was another one of her lovers. You have to feel a bit sorry for Mr. Canning for, when eventually he did become Prime Minister, half the Cabinet refused to serve under him and his term of office lasted for only 118 days. Then he died.

But let us return to this matter of duelling. I had no comprehension of the aristocratic need to prove a man is not afraid to die for a principle. Deliberately missing a rival is frowned upon but honour is satisfied if a man's blood is spilled. Women rarely attended such engagements as men believe they would instantly faint at the merest sight of blood; our monthly bleeding and giving birth goes unacknowledged. Michael strove to instruct me further in the principles of duelling giving the example of two French men settling their differences by shooting at each other's hot air balloons. Both fell to the ground and were killed.

Finding the whole business completely repellent, I stoutly protested when Michael seemed determined to force me to accompany him. I'd become aware of an insidious change in his demeanour toward me lately which made horrid sense when he brusquely revealed he was aware of my impersonation of Hannah Murphy.

I sat in silence as he threatened, 'Either you come with me to support my brother or I will ruin your wonderful career and tell everyone the truth which is - you are an absolute nobody named Elizabeth Taylor. I know full well how much you enjoy your London life but make no mistake, it would take but a word from me for it all to disappear, my dear little Lizzie.'

This duplicitous man I'd believed to be my friend had known I was an imposter from the very day I'd turned up at Drury Lane Theatre; no wonder he'd laughed at me. Not only had he worked with the real Hannah before, he'd also purloined one of the many letters delivered to the theatre from Rev. Coltman addressed to 'Miss Elizabeth Taylor'. Mam was never one for writing. Michael had kept quiet about my deceit until he found the best way of using it to his advantage.

'I know it's commonplace here to invent lies but this is one of the best ever,' he said, maliciously adding, 'And, I hope you are aware, an Act of Parliament is needed for anyone to change their name.'

His callous threats quite shocked and disappointed me. After escaping the domination of Mr. Richard Fox I was appalled to find myself coming under the control of yet another tyrant. What was I to do? Would I risk ruining my position in the theatre? I'd found such delight in acting and the independence a substantial wage had brought me. I concluded I had little option but to go along with him to the duel without knowing exactly why it was so important for me to be there. Therefore, as soon as it was getting light that very next morning, Michael and I were en route by carriage to Putney Heath.

It seemed everything was mustered against Mr. Canning that morning. Lord Castlereagh had the advantage of choosing the place of the contest, near a cottage belonging to his friend and second,

Lord Yarmouth and, as he'd already fought a duel, he knew the procedure exactly.

George Canning clearly expected the worst outcome. Sheepishly he told us not only had he written his will but also a farewell letter to his wife concluding, 'I hope I've made you a happy mother and a proud widow.' That renowned caustic wit that 'could lash the hide off a rhinoceros' seemingly melted into the morning mist.

Ever the betting man, Michael wagered a large sum on Mr. Canning wounding Lord Castlereagh and promised me a share his winnings providing I pulled down my chemise to expose my breasts the very second his lordship took aim. Incredibly this was why Michael considered my presence to be essential - he believed the divulgence of my feminine appendages would distract Lord Castlereagh and so win him his bet. Once more he threatened to tell the Drury Lane Theatre Company I was receiving my wages by deception by impersonating Miss Hannah Murphy. I felt helpless.

Mr. Canning had asked Michael to be his second but he'd ducked out at the last minute saying he could see no point in it. A second has to make sure the event is carried out honourably but that could never sit well with Michael's ethics. His wish to be by my side was purely to ensure I carried out his bidding. Eventually a Mr. Ellis was inveigled into stepping in to take up the position of second. His hat, well pulled down over his face, caused him difficulty in loading the pistol. The impeccably groomed Lord Yarmouth then took over and with a great show of huffing, he thrust the ramrod firmly down both muzzles.

Visibly shaking, Mr. Canning's fingers lacked sufficient control for unfastening his buttons so we helped him off with his greatcoat. The lightening sky revealed his rosebud lips had lost their colour but whether the cool morning air or downright fear caused his shivering, I cannot tell you. He was given first choice of the guns which, being identical, made absolutely no difference.

Mr. C. nodded solemnly as he listened to instructions about the procedure to be followed while Lord Castlereagh irritatingly hummed tunelessly to himself. Off the gentlemen strode until twelve paces apart, they turned, waiting until the handkerchief dropped signalling time to fire. As my hands flew in readiness to the top of my gown, I saw George Canning's shot ping off one of the brass buttons on Lord C.'s fine wool claret jacket and bounce down to the ground. Simultaneously Lord Castlereagh had also fired, before I had any chance to chill my breasts in the morning air.

Blood spread rapidly across Mr. Canning's breeches from being hit at the top of his left thigh. He later fathered four children so clearly no great harm was done to that area. His hat rolled into the dust as he sat down suddenly on the ground, exposing his pale balding head to the rising sun. Followed by Michael, I rushed across to him with the greatcoat to wrap around him

Michael was saying, 'George, George, are you alright? How the devil did you miss him?' And George was saying, 'Zounds, I didn't miss him. I hit his damned button didn't I? I've never held a bloody pistol before in my life. How was I to know it would kick about like that!'

Ripping a piece out of my petticoat I urged him to 'lie back and keep still while I wrap this round your leg and we'll get the doctor across.' Mr. Canning grabbed hold of our outstretched hands and we hoisted him up against a tree, still shocked and trembly. Men began to crowd round proffering smelling salts and poultices. The appointed surgeon dashed across but Mr. C. refused to have his blood let, saying he wanted to hang on to what he still had. We bundled him into his coach and travelled back with him to Gloucester Lodge in Brompton to his anxious wife.

Mr. Canning begged me to tell no one about what had happened; with several sovereigns pressed into my hand I gladly agreed. Everyone present gave a solemn promise to forget they had witnessed the 'affair of honour' knowing otherwise they could be charged as accomplices. Michael came off best as, mendaciously, he sold the full story to a newspaper enabling him to pay off his bet and have plenty left over.

It turned out he'd had a standing arrangement for years with the 'Morning Post' to deposit real or imagined information about the rich and famous into one of their 'Secret Post Boxes'. If it was actually Michael who invented the foul tales they printed about

Lord Nelson and Lady Hamilton and other eminent personages, I would not have been surprised. That same newspaper described the Castlereagh and Canning duel as 'the height of absurdity' and commented, 'Luckily both had resigned from government otherwise what would become of the dignity and authority of Government?' Custom dictates reconciliation should occur if both duellists survive, but there was never a chance of that with these two.

It appeared the King expressed a wish for the whole Tory Cabinet to meet a bloody end and personally sent for Mr. Canning to ascertain whether the wound could possibly prove fatal. Needless to say, Michael kept his wager quiet from his brother, nor did he share the proceeds with me. Oh yes, Mrs. Siddons how correct you were to warn me that 'men, for the most part, are vested with peculiarly lying equivocations.' In other words, women should never put their trust in them.

By persuading myself that Michael would be a dangerous enemy, I decided to stay on friendly terms with him. Despite knowing he was not to be trusted I still found him very entertaining, particularly when he told me more about his extensive family. Apparently after George Canning's father died, his mother had borne ten children, fathered by two different actors. Like Michael, several of them had connections to the theatre; George Canning had the advantage of possessing a rich uncle who had stumped up for a superior education for him at Eton and Oxford, opening the door into politics. Perhaps Mr. Canning expressed his theatricality with his dramatic speeches in the House of Commons. For 'All the world's a stage' as Mr. Shakespeare so rightly says.

Lord Castlereagh, with all his money and power, ended up cutting his own throat. He'd told King George he was being blackmailed for being a bit of a dandy. But would that drive a rich man to suicide? Anyone succeeding at suicide was labelled a lunatic and but failing in the attempt made you a criminal. Although lavish funerals for suicides were unusual, Lord Castlereagh's was held in Westminster Abbey with full ceremony, marred by loud booing echoing around his coffin. His death attracted many nasty comments such as, 'Posterity will ne'er survey a nobler grave than this. Here lie the bones of Castlereagh, Stop traveller and piss.' And even Percy

Bysshe Shelley wrote 'I met murder on the way, He had a mask like Castlereagh.'

The drama of the duel was soon over-shadowed by the magnificence of the King's Jubilee celebrations. When not needed at the theatre Michael and I would take a wherry across the river to enjoy the concerts in Vauxhall Gardens, magical in the dusk when all the lamps were lit. Who cared if it was the wrong year for jubilations; in 1809 King George hadn't actually reigned for the full fifty years? But no one needs an excuse to let off squibs and crackers so processions and celebratory dinners carried on regardless of precise dates. A rare letter from Mam described how guns and bells in Beverley waking them up at midnight on the 24th October particularly enraged Pa; any Royal celebrations inevitably offended his republican tendencies.

The bit I knew about politics mostly came from Pa. From front to back, he would read any newspaper he found. His Radicalism was constantly inflamed by the unfairness of the Corn Laws and lack of universal suffrage and just about everything in the country. He'd say 'That lot in the House of Commons – a lot of useless dummies, voting for whatever their party wants. I tell you, a complete change in the way we're governed is the only answer.'

I don't know what Pa would have said if he'd visited Downing Street as I did with Michael. Our government were certainly not spending our taxes on its upkeep judging by its run-down appearance. Since Mr. Pitt the Younger had died there, the place was just used as offices and for meetings. A Prime Minister could not be expected to live in such shoddy surroundings while magnificent town houses were springing up all over London.

The war had brought so much wealth and power to landowners and manufacturers they competed to have the most fashionable town house money could buy. Money means nothing to those who have it. The National Debt had reached over £500 million so who cared what anyone spent? Not only were fashionable private dwellings being erected but impressive official buildings like the Bank of England and the Royal Hospital. Public buildings like those for the military or navy were mostly being funded by a pernicious Coal Tax, inevitably bringing more hardship to the poor in their crowded, damp houses.   Witnessing the difference between the extravagant lives of the upper classes and the suffering and degradation of the poor made it palpably obvious that I should set myself to acquire capital whenever possible.

When Michael told me the news about the Royal Opera House at Covent Garden burning to the ground, I was totally wretched. Everyone knows how susceptible theatres are to flames and, tragically, twenty-three firemen died when fighting that particular blaze.   In recognition of the fact that theatres were absolutely essential to the happiness of the city, the foundation stone of the new Covent Garden Theatre was laid by the Prince of Wales by the end of the year.   And faster than anyone could believe possible, it was rebuilt and re-opened.

However, when the public discovered the price of tickets for the new boxes had gone up from 6/- to 7/- a massive outcry erupted. Ear-splitting shouts for 'old prices' were drowned out by ever louder trumpets and whistles.   Furious theatre-goers went so far as to release pigeons into the auditorium disrupting performances inducing John Kemble to recant and agree to drop his prices. How satisfying it was to see what power people can wield when working together.

Because of their popularity, the Royal Opera House and Drury Lane Theatre were allowed to keep open throughout the winter. The additional heating and lighting brought added danger to such buildings. How perspicacious it was for Mr. Sheridan to insist on installing an iron safety curtain and water tanks above the stage at Drury Lane.

Chapter 6

A Fire and a Sad Farewell to London

Unfortunately, it was the fire at Drury Lane Theatre that occasioned my return to Beverley. Being so soon after the razing to the ground of Covent Garden, it came as no great surprise to anyone despite Mr. Sheridan's expensive precautions.

On the day of the dreadful fire, I'd returned to the theatre as the sky was darkening and the oil lamps were being lit along Oxford Street. Rather than continue aimlessly meandering about the shops, I resolved to return to the comfort of my dressing room, put my feet up, perhaps getting my maid to put my hair into papillotes before taking my time to dress for the next performance. In hindsight I recognise this as a time when I was supremely happy. As I was singing in 'The Circassian Bride' it was essential to prepare my voice to be heard above the sound effects. Lacking the energy to go about pounding leeks for their juices to mix with honey as commonly advised for 'mellifluous resonance', I decided to make do with tea.

Before crowds arrive, the theatre possesses an eerie stillness and my footsteps echoed unnaturally loudly as I stepped along the passageway. The prospect of meeting the ghost of the Grey Man in his tricorn hat, as described by Mrs. Siddons, suddenly felt very real. As I entered my dressing room my heart almost stopped as someone leapt upon me from behind my dressing screen. I was seized and forcefully pushed down on to the day bed; a hand stifled the screams I was bursting to make. 'Keep quiet Lizzie! It's only me, your friend Michael. How could you be scared of me?'

Once he had removed his hand, I bawled at him, 'What in worlds name do you think you're doing? How dare you scare me half to death, you absolute blackguard.'

'You're not in any position to speak to me like that, Lizzie. Remember you would be wise not to fall out with me when I know so much about you,' he spoke directly into my ear making it warm and damp.

I pushed away his hand, struggling to sit up and keep my equilibrium. I managed, 'Why would you wish to disoblige me like this Michael? I've always believed us to be the best of friends,' after rapidly debating within myself as to which sort of response would be in my best interest.

'Oh but I feel now we should become so much more dear Lizzie,' said Michael, pressing me down again, his onion-flavoured breath brought me to the verge of vomiting.

'In London my name is Hannah,' I reminded him.

'I would rather like to think of you as my Queen Caroline and I can be your own Bartolomeo.' And he produced one of those cartoons you see plastered all over the windows of Drury Lane Print Shop for 7/6d; this one was crumpled having been bought cheaply from a friend. I had no wish to see the exposed flesh and lewd words purporting to belong to the Queen and her manservant portrayed behaving in such an unseemly, debauched manner. Pushing the print in front of my face he replaced his lips against my ear and read those salacious words to me. He licked my lobe.

'Come now Lizzie we could enjoy ourselves like them. It would make your best friend very happy and he would probably forget all about Lizzie Taylor and it's just possible he would become Hannah Murphy's humble servant once more.'

Perhaps it would have been easier to submit to him but I feared this wouldn't be the end and Michael would continue to make even more obscene demands. And wasn't it just conceivable the Drury Lane Company would value me enough to ignore my imposture or even proclaim it as an audacious jape by their leading lady?

As Michael's fetid palm crept up to my garter, I brought my knee forcefully to where I knew it would hurt him most, managing to pull away from his grasp. Perchance if I hadn't fought off Michael's horrid attack, the candle would never have been knocked over. It set alight the trailing edge of my sleeve before igniting the curtain as I tried to put out furious flames springing up around me.

Was I to blame or should the true blame lie with the threadbare trash in the newspapers? Or perhaps with the printmakers and their endless reporting of the licentious activities of Queen Caroline and her 'servant' Bartolomeo Pergami? Like so many men, Michael had become absolutely obsessed by those caricatures of the Queen naked to the waist. On previous occasions I had laughed away his efforts to persuade me to re-enact such debauchery even when he resorted to assuring me that such experiences were essential for me to bring a true understanding to the characters I was required to play on stage.

Until his half-brother's duel with Lord Castlereagh fiasco had brought me such disenchantment, I really had considered Michael my true friend. Trying to coerce me into uncovering my breasts to distract Lord Castlereagh and then making money by selling the story to the Morning Post caused me to realise Michael's complete lack of integrity. His knowledge of my true identity convinced him I had no option other than become his submissive mistress.

But what really convinced me he was a jack-pudding was at that very moment the flames seized hold of my trailing sleeve, he callously abandoned me to the fire. Screaming and furious that my precious gown was being destroyed, I was left alone to rapidly divest myself. I'd really loved that chemise, delicately embroidered with tiny silver sprigs; you never see such beautiful tambour work nowadays.

Leaving the inferno behind to devour the rest of the dressing room, I snatched my wrap and chased up to the stage, ignoring the pain of my burned arm. There I found Mr. Richard Sheridan installed in front of the safety curtain, wineglass in hand, inspecting the properties and scenery. Hearing my screams of 'Help! Fire!' and discerning my distress, he said 'Why it's the lady who knows nothing of Molière!' He seized my hand, pulling me along the passageway. Out on the safety of Drury Lane I was astounded to see he'd barely spilled a drop of his Madeira. After standing stock still, regarding the smoke and flames, he calmly turned to the gathering crowd and declaimed, 'A man may surely be allowed to take a glass of wine by his own fireside do you not think?' Blasé, that's the French word for him.

Richard Sheridan was such a talented man. What a joy it had been for me to play Lady Teazle in his 'School for Scandal'. Screams of laughter from the gallery and the pit would ring out at the clever way Mr. Sheridan captured the popular view of polite society. You'd hear little merriment issuing from the boxes however, as it seemed beyond the wit of the monied classes to comprehend jokes about their pretentious existence. The commonalty were Richard Sheridan's keenest enthusiasts.

Last century he'd been a Member of Parliament. Michael Macready told me that even there he'd done his best to entertain his audience. When Edmund Burke had thought it essential to alert the House to the danger of England being invaded by French Revolutionaries, to emphasise his point he'd hurled a knife down on to the floor of the House. Whereupon Mr. Sheridan had yelled 'Where's the fork?' Mr. Burke's dire warnings were overwhelmed by guffaws and completely ignored.

Remorse wells up inside me even now, when I reflect on how, quite accidentally, I brought that excellent man, Richard Sheridan, to ruin. Having effectively burnt my boats as well as a theatre it seemed a judicious time to return to Yorkshire.

What a difference turnpikes made to travel and now we even have the luxury of railway trains! No more getting out and walking up the hills to save the horses, thank the Lord. I forget who told me of a blind man called Jack Metcalfe who once walked from London to Yorkshire in sixty hours, far faster than coaches managed on the old roads.

The prospect of another wearisome journey filled me with dismay and you may be forgiven for wondering why I would contemplate dashing back to Beverley. However, after the strain of the past months I longed for something more mundane. I slept soundly at every coaching inn despite the badness of the beds and the closeness of the rooms. This time my journey took me through the delightfully named Biggleswade and then up to Peterborough and

Lincoln. Over innumerable hills of minor altitude I arrived at Barton where for the first time, I risked boarding the Royal Charter Steam Packet across to Kingston- upon-Hull. A coach setting off from Hull's famous Land of Green Ginger, jumbled me back to Beverley just before it grew dark.

The town was much the same as I'd left it whereas I knew I was completely changed both in confidence and appearance. I got down at the Golden Fleece. I paid a lad to carry my bag which Mam told me was money misspent, and took trouble to persuade me I was trying to exalt myself above my station in life. It was now an effort for her to even boil a kettle for tea as she had become too wide for her narrow kitchen being twice the width of Pa. She breathed heavily on moving but he still scuttled around the town carpentering and building; his face webbed with wrinkles excluded all emotion.

Mam and Pa seemed surprised rather than pleased to see me. They didn't care for my new clothes; said I looked a baggage. To avoid a wrangle over my purchase of some stylish sealskin boots, I told them that one of the actresses in the company had given them to me for arranging her hair. I didn't wish my parents to know just how much I'd been paid as the famous actress Hannah Murphy. All my stories of London or the people I'd met elicited nothing but scorn.

My mother perfected her tutting to a fine art while my father had no comprehension of how any man, particularly an old soldier, could miss shooting a king at such close quarters. He showed me his old gun to explain to me exactly what James Hadfield should have done to steady his hand. Mam kept shushing him, afraid he would be hung for treason if he was heard saying such a thing.

Pa's republican opinions caused him to rail privately against the appointment of a Prince Regent. His argument was that even a mad king who had lost us America was better than a fat, greedy womaniser who refused to contemplate the emancipation of the Catholics. A Revolution such as that in France bringing an end to aristocratic rule would certainly be a good idea here and Pa could definitely see why Napoleon with his modest beginnings, was so popular in France.

'Just listen to this Mother and our Lizzie', Pa yelled as he came home one evening, 'That Tom Fool Sir Masterman Sykes is so sure Mr. Napoleon Bonaparte will soon be assassinated, he says until that happens, he'll pay a sovereign a day to anyone who thinks different and is prepared to stake fifty guineas to back their belief. The Emperor's a hero, no one would kill him.'

'Happen Sir Masterman will have to hire someone to shoot Boney then to save him losing the bet,' said Mam, 'I would if I'd more money than sense like them lot up at Sledmere House.' Pa just sniffed, he never aimed at wit.

Of course, we now know that didn't happen and the Clergyman who took on the ridiculous wager made hundreds of pounds until the bet was called off, which was lucky for Sir Masterman as the 'Corsican Monster' carried on for years after that. Everyone had thought it was all up with him once the Allies had him locked up in a castle on the island of Elba. Who would have believed they would allow him to carry on being an Emperor and recruit his own little army and navy? Of course he would take the opportunity to sally back to rule France once more. But it was only a few months before our good old Duke of Wellington saw to him good and proper and got him shut up on the Isle of St. Helena just that bit further away.

Other conversations with my father mostly concerned the alterations at the Minster Vicarage which Pa had been employed to carry out before the Rev. Coltman could move in. He'd been living at Amphion House in North Bar Without but was finding it increasingly arduous to propel his gargantuan body along on his hobby horse to the Minster.

Pa's complaint was that too much of his time was being wasted by the Vicar exchanging what he regarded as a few pleasantries whereas Pa saw them as plain annoyances. He needed to concentrate on meticulous measurement of doorways and floors previous to him widening and strengthening them with timber beams to cater for the Vicar's great girth. Mr. Coltman still must come backwards down the stairs so he could see them.

The Vicar asked Pa to accompany him to the Great West Door of the Minster and inspect the old wood for bullets after discovering a strange story in the course of his historical research. It seems Oliver Cromwell's soldiers during the Civil War had used the West door for target practice and fired their muskets at it.

'Looks like there's quite a few pitted in there,' says Pa to the Vicar, 'Hurrah for the Roundheads', carelessly showing his anti-Royalist tendencies whilst wishing to get on with his work. This didn't sit well with the Vicar who put him right saying, 'Ah but Mr. Taylor, a vision of our beloved St. John appeared to them and scared them all away so evidently he was supporting the King.'

After that Pa realised he should keep his opinions to himself about the Church and Royalty whilst at the Vicarage so as not to hazard his employment there. However, such pent-up frustration drove him to let rip at me and Mam once he got home. With no wish to hear our opinions, he just took the opportunity to discharge his anger into any available ear. Selfishly I just gave up listening to Pa's rants.

Perhaps going back home was a mistake. The town seemed very dreary and I found the foul smells worsened by Mr. Hodgson's even larger tannery on Flemingate. If you went across to the other side of town on a Wednesday you'd get the stink from the cattle brought in to the market on Norwood. I found such onslaughts on my nose vastly more objectionable than all the street smells of London.

One afternoon I trudged into town to see how the demolition of the old Newbegin Bar was getting on. It had been in a precarious condition for as long as I could remember. When I espied Mary Ann Salmond coming toward me, I prepared myself for stopping to gossip. But no, she merely bestowed the slightest nod to me as we passed. Although we'd been close friends at school, I knew she had recently inherited a huge house in North Bar Street, so was obviously far too grand now for the likes of me. I smiled to myself; how could she or anyone else have supposed that only one month ago, dressed in the latest fashion, I was being applauded by massive audiences in the capital city of England?

It took but a few weeks of ostracism and criticism in Beverley to determine me to leave and find somewhere more welcoming to a single independent 'lady'. Not being answerable to anyone else is a tremendous blessing so long has you have no fear. Mr. Percy Shelley's words, 'Beware for I am fearless therefore powerful,' I decided to adopt as my motto.

For the past few years, I'd confidently conversed with the rich and famous and dealt with several unexpected situations. Therefore, with only slight trepidation and Mam and Pa offering little encouragement to me to stay, I set off on a solitary journey back down to London. Though I became well acquainted with the coach I found little congenial conversation with fellow passengers. Urchins ran out shouting and waving as we passed through villages; I waved back graciously. When I tired of my book, I fixed my gaze at church spires peering over dense green yew trees or fields of oats being sown. You have no notion of how many shades of soil exist in our country.

These diversions left me plenty of time to spend on planning a future quite unconnected to theatricals. I recalled how Mr. Canning had complained of his desperate search for a reliable housekeeper for his new house, therefore it occurred to me this indicated a scarcity of women suitable for such employment in London. I determined to visit one of those agencies that provided servants for the grander mansions.

At the second coaching inn of the journey, I obtained paper and quill and set myself to produce a glowing character reference for myself. I perfected Mr. Fox's particular flourish to reproduce his signature below my claims of being entirely respectable and trustworthy. There was little point going back to Drury Lane Theatre for a recommendation. No one there could vouch for my honesty and reliability now I'd reclaimed my given name and Hannah Murphy had virtually disappeared from the face of the earth. Unfortunately, it turned out I couldn't ask my next employer, Mr. Bellingham for a reference when subsequent events conspired to my losing my place with him.

Chapter 7

In Which Mr. John Bellingham's Story is Told

The Domestic Servants Intelligence Office I approached had, that very day, received an urgent plea for a housekeeper from a Mr. John Bellingham. The Agency despatched me to a small but elegant house quite close to the River Thames, the rented home of Mr. Bellingham and Mary, his wife. Their real home was Liverpool.

They lived ill together. She wasn't much for housekeeping, preferring to occupy herself with magazines such as 'La Belle Assemblèe' all day long. I was left to my own devices, organising the household and doing a bit of plain work. Every now and again there Mrs. B. would go, flitting around her husband with a caressing fondness from which he abruptly turned his head, causing her to flounce from the room. I always found him quite congenial. His honest round pale grey eyes peered out from an unfurrowed face, unless he was telling you of his misfortunes. Only then would he pull down the corners of his mouth and wipe away a supposed tear.

'You know Eliza,' he always called me Eliza. 'You would not believe the troubles I've had.' And I'd take a seat and sit back, hoping he would unburden himself for I love a good story, but we'd usually find ourselves discussing general matters of the moment.

Catholic Emancipation was all the talk at that time. Mr. Bellingham harboured strong objections to such an idea as did Beverley Corporation who petitioned Parliament nine times against giving more rights to Catholics. I was pleased when Mr. William Wilberforce changed his mind on the matter and came to agree with me that people should be free to worship as they saw fit. After all, I agreed with him on the matter of abolishing slavery. I'd listened to Reverend Coltman preaching, 'we must consider Christianity at war with the principle and practice of slavery'. The swelling desire for freedom and equality for slaves and Catholics, while admirable, still held out little hope for changing the status of us women.

Mr. Bellingham was an undemanding employer and very generous with his money. I got 1/- a week plus what I could make on the side of course. He entrusted me with the keys and I hired in girls to do the washing, ironing and mending and a bit of cooking. I had an allowance to pay them although obviously, they only got a half of what he was prepared to pay as I made sure to first deduct my agent's fee. I did consent to wait on table; I relished the entertainment of listening to my employers' snappish exchanges.

Eventually one evening, I did discover more of his story after Mrs. B. had retired to her chamber; she was always having bilious attacks. I blamed that awful Fowler's Solution she took after every meal; I'd warned her it contained arsenic. Mr. B. at last got away from speaking in ambiguities and around to telling me the cause of his misfortunes. He'd had quite a bit to drink; never being quite the five-bottle man he thought he was. Responding to my enquiring demeanour Mr. Bellingham disclosed he'd been imprisoned in Russia for some time which, I surmised, was the reason he'd lost touch with what had been going on in England. He certainly didn't have much idea of the cost of groceries thank the Lord.

'Now why in heaven's name would you go all that way to Russia?' I asked him. I knew it was a long way because I'd located the country on the globe in the drawing room. Always enjoying hearing about foreign countries, I continued to encourage him to tell me about what Russian folk ate and their mode of dress but most of all about his prison life.

He shook his head. 'I really don't want to talk about it, Eliza, it's too, too painful. All I want now is three good meals a day, fresh white shirts and clean bed linen. Is that too much to ask?'

It was quite a lot to ask in actual fact, wanting seven shirts a week called for cauldrons of hot water, the soap, the bleach, the starch, mangling, heating the irons and so on but what would a man know of that business? Not that I knew that much about it either for in order to leave a greater margin for me from the housekeeping accounts, I'd begun to cut down on the groceries, resulting in a lack of sufficient flour to make the starch for all those shirts.

On opposing sides of the fireplace that evening, he gradually got over his reluctance to speak about his past and poured out his tales of woe. I must admit I felt a bit sorry for the old sod and if he was handing me a bag of moonshine, what did I care? If only half of what he said was true, you would have to admire Mr. Bellingham. He'd been a jeweller, a sailor and even ran a tin factory for a time until his 'enemies', as he called them, conspired to bring about his ruin.

'All my working life you know Eliza, I've nurtured this strong obligation to work hard for my country. My remarkable success in improving European trade naturally emboldened me to strike ever further afield. Some ship owners of my acquaintance persuaded me to establish a business relationship with some Russian fellows on their behalf. All that way to Russia I went on that very errand but did they thank me for it? No, they did not,' he said loudly, clearing a phlegmy throat.

'People can be so very ungrateful,' I consoled.

'Quite so! All my adult life I can assure you, I've been unstinting in my efforts to support this country's interests. My greatest mistake was having an invincible belief that every British citizen should account for something in this world. I'm sure you've heard of that fellow, Mr. David Pacifico? And you can't even call that a good English name can you? Not like Bellingham or Taylor, eh? Well, he made such a dust about a mob burning down his house in Athens, he got Lord Palmerston to order our English Navy to blockade the harbour there because those old Greeks wouldn't give him the compensation he demanded. And he got every bit of his money back, so why should I not get something back for being penned up at the Tsar of Russia's pleasure? After all, I was only there to improve British trade!'

'What you should do is petition the Foreign Secretary to put your case to the Russians,' I said, feeling it incumbent upon me to provide a clear insight of the best way to achieve what he wanted.

'Obviously I would not expect a woman to keep up with affairs of state,' Mr. Bellingham gently scoffed. 'You cannot be aware that our confounded British Government decided to break off diplomatic relations with those damned Ruskies at the very moment I needed them most. And Mary doesn't help, she continually reminds me I'm the author of my own misfortunes'.

'Oh, Mr. Bellingham however could she believe such a thing?' I cried, persisting in making a conspicuous effort to show how much I was taking his part.

'Well, to be completely honest with you, the trouble actually arose when Lloyds of London received anonymous information about a certain ship being deliberately sunk in the White Sea; its owners were making a massive insurance claim for its accidental loss. How they discovered I was the informer I cannot tell you but when those ship owners found out they were incensed. They maliciously told the Russian government that I was in arrears to them for a vast amount of roubles; that's the Russian currency you know. The sole reason I was put into that prison was for a fictitious, non-existent debt.'

During this long soliloquy his beer went from foam to flat but it was good to keep him away from the black bile which laid him low from time to time. To bring our conversation away from the catastrophe of a sinking ship and to happier considerations, I asked, 'But you are here now Mr. Bellingham, so now you must tell me, how did you manage to get your freedom back?'

'Eliza, incredibly, it was the Tsar of Russia himself who responded to my pleas. Nothing whatever to do with our dastardly, corrupt Government.' Mr. Bellingham knocked back the last of his ale, slamming down his tankard.

Again, purely to keep his spirits high, I empathised, urging him to recommence his petitions to various Members of Parliament because of course being a British citizen should account for something in this world. I said it was essential to create a great fuss about injustice. After Mr. Bellingham's particular ranting about the 'obnoxious and ill-informed' Mr. George Canning, I kept the information that I was acquainted with him to myself. However together we concluded that every individual Minister should be held responsible for the many shortcomings of the government and that Mr. B. should petition them all.

I often went to the House of Commons with him on that very errand, intrigued to see the place where all the great debates and decisions were made. I just wish they would make all their decisions based on Mr. Jeremy Bentham's enlightened proposition that only laws bringing most happiness to most people should be passed.

Smartly arrayed in his dark brown tail coat with velvet collar, John Bellingham would accost any Member who met his eye and endeavour to present his petition. He said little when rebuffed but plenty once at home when he would carry on ranting over the unfairness of life. He reserved a particularly strong dislike of the Prime Minister, Mr. Spencer Percival. I know Mr. Canning also despised him; he'd refused to become his Foreign Secretary so long as Lord Castlereagh remained in his Cabinet. How we laughed at reading the reports of Mr. Perceval declaring himself completely against hunting, drinking and adultery. As Mr. Bellingham said, having fathered 14 children, he would have had little time for such diversions in any case.

Over the years I have found I'm very good at getting men into a particular mood by asking apposite questions. I would say to Mr. Bellingham 'Tell me more about the House of Commons, I've heard it called a 'temple of the movers and shakers.' The people there must be so clever.'

That would get him warmed up immediately, 'What a fool' he'd say about Mr. Perceval. 'And just why does he want to pursue this ridiculous war in Europe? Making friends with other countries is what we should be doing.' And 'Why does he not see that he should be helping those people who put their lives in danger in order to improve overseas trade? Ministers should never be able to turn their backs and pretend they know nothing.' He became so beguiled by the earnestness of his belief that it progressed to him deciding that the only solution would be to rid the land of such a man as Spencer Perceval and he was the fellow to do it.

You may be sure I agreed with his every word. I humoured him by describing how King George was almost killed in Drury Lane Theatre and what my father had said about successfully shooting people, offering his advice on the best guns to purchase for assassinations. I even took it upon myself to sew a sturdy hidden pocket into his new jacket to accommodate his pistols despite my hatred of needlework. And so the assassination of the Prime Minister came to pass.

Being unsure how Mrs. Bellingham would react to being informed of her husband's arrest, I took refuge in a Coaching Inn for two nights after the event before approaching her about retaining my position in her household. Her blank face and shaken head informed me she'd no intention of employing me again. She was no longer the irresolute sloth I'd thought her to be, for with a dismissive shrug she closed the door right in my face. I believe by then Mrs. Bellingham was already aware that the public subscription raised for her support had awarded her more money than she'd ever seen in her life. Within the year she'd remarried, left London and moved on from her life with the 'lunatic'.

However, I resolved to remain in the same area, strangely comforted by the familiarity of the smell and the sounds from the River Thames. With a little luck and asking about, I found a nice situation with a neighbour of Mr. Bellingham, Mr. Holloway. He had always given me the time of day whenever we met in the street, doffing his hat to air prominent eyebrows juxtaposed above a hooked nose. Quite the flamboyant man about town, he was employed by Paxtons Bank in Pall Mall. He advised people to get rich by investing in the gold and silver mines of South America but appeared unscathed by the usual heart-hardening effect of commerce. I settled in comfortably and did a bit of housekeeping for him and such.

It was Mr. Holloway who taught me the waltz. After I'd let slip that I loved to dance, he took me along to some Assembly Rooms. How shocked Mam would have been to see an unmarried woman like me held so closely by a man in public; I found it very enjoyable despite the presence of the nose jutting over my shoulder.

After dinner one evening Mr. Holloway invited me to sit with him in his drawing room saying, 'Could we have a word, Miss Murphy?' I'd given him my stage name for two reasons. Firstly, I wished to disconnect myself from any connection to John Bellingham and secondly, I'd surmised I would appear more interesting if I could speak freely of my theatrical triumphs.

'Now, how'd you like to earn a bit of real money for yourself?' He smiled at the way his question made my eyes light up. I never needed asking twice to add to my bank account. At opposite sides of the rosewood tea table, I listened as he explained, 'I must assure you that this is just a bit of a lark that some of my friends have come up with, no harm to anyone, I do assure you. I took the liberty of suggesting to them that you would be the perfect person to help us get our faradiddle believed, considering your splendid reputation as an actress.'

I smiled complacently at the compliment as he instructed me, 'All we wish you to do, early next Monday morning, is to dash into the smartest shops, the coffee houses and chocolate houses around Town, just as many as you can possibly manage. Once through each door you must shout as loudly but as convincingly as possible, "Wonderful news! Napoleon is dead! The Bourbons are back in charge of France." Then you scurry on to the next such establishment and do the same again.' Mr. Holloway said, if challenged, I could explain that my employer had heard all about it through the semaphore telegraph and had urged me to do my best to spread the splendid news around the town.

On the specified morning, I wrapped up warmly in my black silk pelisse trimmed with white fur, as from a mouse-brown sky, flakes of snow had slowly been fluttering. I got one of the maids to arrange my curls over my forehead and ears, looking all the crack with the real Hannah's ermine muff.

You would not believe how happy I made everyone. The horrors of war having caused so many tears and privations, were supplanted by joy, cheering, handshaking and back-slapping. As I dashed into more Coffee and Chocolate Houses awash with old maids and old bachelors, all avid for gossip, the easier it got. By mid-morning, I was just screeching 'Boney's dead!' through every door leaving the clientele congratulating one another and spreading the news for themselves.

And Mr. Holloway of course was delighted with me. He gave me 100 guineas just for spreading good news, can you believe that? How was I to know it was all a fudge having not enough shrewdness in my nature to realise his true intentions.

It turned out that Mr. Holloway and several of his friends had been buying up a lot of Government trading stocks in the week before, at fairly low cost to themselves. That Monday, as news of Napoleon Bonaparte's death rapidly spread throughout London, prices rocketed up and Mr. Holloway's friends and those in the know happily sold their stocks for over a million pounds. Later that afternoon as no dispatches had been received to confirm the victory, doubts crept in and Government stocks fell like a rock. Although it was a trickster called Colonel du Bourg who received most of the blame for spreading the pernicious rumours, it seems many others were driven by cupidity, including my Mr. Holloway.

As more of the story emerged you had to marvel at the intricacies of the plot. It turned out that a person dressed as a military officer had landed at Dover before going about the town announcing he was the bearer of the exciting news of Napoleon Bonaparte being hacked to pieces by a group of Cossack soldiers. That 'officer' then travelled by post-chaise and four, dropping similar hints at every staging post before arriving at Lord Cochrane's mansion in Grosvenor Square. Being such a well-respected Member of Parliament and Naval hero, his announcement about an Allied Victory in France bringing an end to the war was believed by everyone.

My exertions around the fashionable parts of the City became even more important to the success of the conspiracy due to the telegraph becoming useless when a thick mist at Deal made the semaphore flags impossible to see. Six of the rascally plotters were charged with fraud and imprisoned. Lord Cochrane was stripped of his knighthood and dismissed from the Navy. The judges decided against putting him into a pillory, afraid his popularity would have led to him being showered with gifts and ever more adulation. His supporters even paid his fine.

I don't really know why there was such a fuss. Maybe most of London was deceived into celebrating the longed-for Peace but it was only one year too early. And as you know, there are always ups and downs in the Stock Market; only about ten years later everything crashed and all those holding mining shares were totally ruined. Needless to say, you should not blame me for the Great Stock Exchange Fraud; I was but an unwitting pawn.

Chapter 8

A Description of Domestic Life

I'm sure you will understand, once I'd received my hundred guineas, I left London. Discreetly inserted in the corner of a carriage full of overgrown men I transposed myself once more to Beverley determined to settle down in my home town this time.

I was slightly unsettled by the delight exhibited by Mr. Fox on my return. The death of old Alice Hardaker, had obliged him to acquire another, even older housekeeper who lived in a tiny room at the back of the shop being unable to manage stairs. Mam and Pa had installed a lodger in my old room and I jibbed at sharing with our Bill so I had little option but to ask Mr. F. if I could be accommodated up in his attic.

'Of course you can my dear Elizabeth, if you can bear to share it with all the spiders and earwigs,' he smirked as he squeezed my arm. 'I've really missed having you here.'

Straightaway I could sense there wouldn't be much time alone in the attic and before long Mr. Fox was urging me to share his own big feather bed once more. He was still fit as a lop. Whether his housekeeper suspected our sleeping arrangements I was unsure, but the sullen silence as I entered any room whenever she was closeted with Mr. Fox caused me to suspect I was interrupting her malicious efforts to disparage me.

Hoping to discomfort her, I conducted myself with overwhelming courtesy in her company, flaunting the new sophisticated southern accent I'd acquired; she remained draggled and dull. I'd already made up my mind it would suit me if she left and, the following week, she was sacked for stealing. Two bottles of sherry wine secreted in her chamber! How despicable! Mr. Fox couldn't abide dishonesty and who could blame him?

The very next morning I was appointed his trusted housekeeper with carte blanche to do the household accounts, manage the shop and employ whoever I thought fit. With my vast experience of running sizeable London households this was no problem to me. I planned to rule the roost. However, two days later it was 'That backyard could do with a good sweep', 'Have you wound the clocks?' 'Where have you been?' and 'Don't you ever forget a farthing a day is seven shillings a year; you'd best be careful with my money!' Had Mr. Fox missed me or just someone else to dictate to? You think you're the queen but find you still have no rights.

Insidiously, our relationship reverted to ten years back. Mr. Fox decided what was best for me, his concern smothered me. 'How ever did you manage to live in London without your friends and family? Totally heartless you were, abandoning everyone who loved you,' was probably his nearest approach to any endearment.

Mr. Fox's manipulation of my days mixed up my head and caused me sleepless nights. In some ways he brought order into my life with his prescriptive duties but doubts kept intruding. How long would this arrangement suit me? The feeling of comfort I was gaining from someone else making my decisions also brought intermittent feelings of despair at my pathetic subordination.

I often reflected on the advice given two years previously by a certain notorious personage I had met in London who knew more than most about such conflictions. Sitting one morning with Michael in the only Chocolate House he identified as being fit for a leading lady such as myself, who should sweep in but Mrs. Maria Fitz-Herbert herself? She appeared delighted when Michael stood up to invite her to join our table flamboyantly introducing me as 'the wondrously talented Miss Hannah Murphy.' She appeared very pleased to meet me, being a great afficionado of the theatre; that was where she and Michael had first become acquainted.

Inevitably, all heads turned to stare at her through the smoke and steam apart from those who could view her via the mirrors lining the walls. Conversation lulled before the chattering crescendoed and crammed the room. Mrs. F-H ignored all the attention she attracted and concentrated on us. She was one of those people you feel instantly drawn to, utterly charming and fascinatingly confiding. With her head inclined close to mine she described her sorrow at being widowed twice within five years whilst quite young. The dreadful thing was that both her husbands had died intestate leaving her in financial difficulties. Who could blame her for being flattered and delighted when noticed by the Prince of Wales?

Despite her 'Prinny' dramatically stabbing himself when she'd refused to become his mistress she clung to her religious beliefs and insisted on their marriage. Ruefully she told me, 'The world is always ready to invent falsehoods about women you know but nevertheless I had no wish to become penniless again!' Aiming to cheer her, I read her coffee grounds, assuring her that the wavy lines I could see in her cup assured her of future happiness and the return of her sweet Prince.

Much was made of the matter in the newspapers. They pointed out that to make the marriage lawful, the King had to give his blessing. This he absolutely refused to do so because Maria was a Commoner and a Catholic. The Prince's official wife, Queen Caroline, must have believed his first marriage to be lawful for she declared at her trial in the House of Lords that the only person she had ever committed adultery with was Mrs. Fitz-Herbert's husband.

Mrs. Fitz-Herbert glanced around the coffee house, affably nodding to several people she recognised. 'It's quite delightful to be sitting here with you like this', she said. 'I'm getting used to simpler forms of entertainment now. Prinny was so extravagant, particularly when he wished to impress. You know when the Tsar of Russia came for dinner at Brighton, George actually ordered the chef to produce one hundred and twenty different dishes including the most wondrous confection of sugar, pastry and marzipan. Without one word of a lie, it was as tall as you.'

My strongest memory of that day was Mrs. Fitz-Herbert tapping my hand as we parted saying, 'Marriage to any rich old man is the most judicious strategy a woman can ever come up with, especially as she grows older. And always make sure you are in your husband's will, my dear.' I'd no wish to walk in her shoes but I knew she was correct. Any sane woman should try to protect herself for a future of deteriorating looks and energy. We can't all achieve the benefit of being made a Duchess after the death of a 'husband' as Mrs. Fitz-Herbert did.

Therefore, reflecting on her advice, I steeled myself to have a serious word with Mr. Fox. 'Now, sir, why don't you and me get wed. Make everything seemly,' I said, very calm and reasonable while snug together in bed one evening.

'What? I do not believe you know what you are saying Elizabeth. I mean we're not what you'd call equals. I have my position in town to think of. Whatever would people say? Nay it's out of the question,' he said belittling me yet again.

'But you use me like a wife, I do everything you ask. Why shouldn't I have a bit of security?' I said, still reasonable.

'Nay lass you've got the wrong end of the stick. I pay you and put a roof over your head and that is why you do as I say. Where would we be if women could say what was what, eh?'

'Just thought you would fancy having an elegant lady hanging on your arm when you attend all your official engagements.' I suggested mildly.

'What a joke that would be, you'd just flaunt off down to London again if things didn't suit, leaving me here looking a bloody old fool. You'll soon lose any security if you push me too far. One word from me and you'd be in the House of Correction for defamation of my character. So just you think on,' said Mr. Fox.

I did think on, turning away from him trying to put some space between us, always difficult in a feather bed with a huge dip in the middle.

Over his shoulder he muttered on - copulation was an aspect of my duty to him but he would call me his wife in private if that would make me happy. On reflection I think he believed himself to be more attractive to his female customers by remaining an eligible bachelor. He was a handsome man still, tall as a Grenadier with lovely thick white hair and not a bit fat on him.

At that time Mr. Fox was paying me well so I concealed my chafed spirits. I accepted my situation having no imperative yet to go elsewhere in search of a suitable husband, after all he'd never struck me. And there was the comfort of knowing I had my Mr. Holloway money safely stashed away behind the fast-bolted, red baize door in Machell's Bank.

I spent a bit of it on some suitable high-necked gowns trimmed with a pretty bit of ribbon and some serviceable dimity aprons for the shop. I daren't get anything too modish for Beverley. None of that showing all you've got, bosoms falling out over the top like they wear in London. No corsets though, not that I'd any need for them never having had a bairn back then.

I'd learned a lot about dressing well to keep up with the other London actresses. When they dedicated a marble plaque to Mr. Samuel Butler at a special service in St. Marys I wore my iris-blue day dress with three bands of ribbons round the hem under my lovely Spencer Jacket with brass buttons that I'd drawn for Mrs. Burton to copy. Mr. Butler was the theatre manager who'd regularly brought his troupe of actors to perform at the Lairgate Theatre. The plaque said something about him being 'a poor player that struts and frets his hour upon the stage and then is heard no more.' That's Shakespeare and actors for you.

At last our true Peace arrived and old Boney was captured; it had certainly taken long enough. The whole country rejoiced and I had the extra gratification of a substantial bank account for simply prematurely announcing such a thing on behalf of Mr. Holloway and his fellow conspirators. Quite inconceivably after all their vicissitudes, those muddle-headed Frenchies decided to put a King back on their throne, despite enduring the privations of a bloody Revolution for years!

'We should get rid of our lot as well!' said Pa, in unusual agreement with Lord Castlereagh who'd got into bother when overheard saying he would drink 'to the rope that should hang the last king.' And him a noble Viscount and all. A bit daft like most other aristocratic representatives of the bourgeoisie in Parliament.

Perhaps it would have been exciting to be still in London to celebrate the Peace and the end of fear and food riots caused by the War. Courtesy of the Prince Regent there was a massive firework display in Hyde Park but the 'Temple of Concord' they'd erected, back lit by several rows of oil lamps did nothing to prevent the amount of fighting and cheating that went on there.

We did our best in Beverley. Church bells rang out around the town, and we were treated to a sight of our principal inhabitants marshalled together with twenty-four constables, banners aloft, processing from the Guild Hall to Wednesday Market Place for the Peace Proclamation. The crowd then drifted on to Saturday Market to be deafened by eight guns giving the Royal Salute. After which everyone sang 'God Save the King' around the Market Cross specially adorned with spirals of coloured lamps and evergreens; even those stone urns perched up on the top were illuminated.

For weeks we had dinners and balls to celebrate our triumph over our French foes. How strange it is to reflect how sworn enemies like Great Britain and France have now become comrades in arms to fight against the Russian threat in Crimea.

Mr. Fox took me to a few dinners at the Hall Garth Inn and the Mucky Duck, otherwise known as the Black Swan. I often excused myself from these outings, finding the whispering behind fans quite put me off my food. Despite that I started to put a bit of weight on.

At one of the feasts where I did put in an appearance, I encountered Gillyatt Sumner, done up like a duke's dinner in his blue tailcoat with gold buttons. Gilly loved to cut a dash with all the fashionable clothes he brought back from Leeds and York; he hoped to turn Beverley into the Bath of the North. He attended every dinner to which he was invited, whether by the Whigs or the Tories, he cared not. He had walked into town from his house in Flemingate in his new Brunswick boots which evidently were now causing him much anguish.

On catching sight of me he caught my arm and, in a theatrically loud whisper, he said 'Come and sit down with me Lizzie; we love a bit of tittle tattle don't we?'

'Why Mr. Sumner,' said I, 'You won't wish to be seen with the likes of me. Think of your reputation!'

'Not at all, not at all, no one is looking and even if they are it'll give them something else to talk about!' he said.

Sitting beside him I soon realised that, as well as resting his feet, what he really wanted was a listening ear for tales of the transgressions of his countless antagonists. Being a burgess as well as landlord of many properties in the town, Gillyatt Sumner involved himself with all levels of society. He'd done very well for himself considering his father was a mere fell monger and skinner. This particular evening, Gilly was in the mood to complain about Mr. John McCue, a tenant who had owed him £1.14s.3d. for two years and been given notice to quit several times. Gillyatt wouldn't accept his excuse that as there was neither a lock nor a key to the door, it was impossible for him to physically hand over the key to his landlord.

The only people Gilly was sure to keep on good terms with were Solicitors, as he regularly engaged them to get redress for unpaid rent or to take action for the numerous times people and their dogs attacked him. He ran close to the Prince of Wales and Lord Castlereagh in his acquisition of enemies for he never felt an obligation to be civil to anyone who was not of use to him.

When I could get a word in edgeways, I tapped his hand with my fan and said lightly, 'Now Mr. Sumner you must tell me the reason for the ill-feeling between you and some of the Churchwardens I keep hearing so much about,' I held my head well back to avoid the inhalation of too much of his eye-watering pomade.

'Never in this world would you wish to know all the dreadful details, dear Lizzie. I must hope to satisfy your curiosity by merely outlining the generally mutinous mood manifesting itself in the Minster. St. Martin's men are monsters.' His eyes danced, impressed by his procession of m's; satire and caricature being his customary pattern of speech.

'But I believed you all to be Christians; surely you are required to be full of love towards your fellow believers?' I pressed him.

'Oh but my dear, I love them all deeply. However, you must understand, this is a Historic Problem and definitely not of my making,' he said, strongly emphasising every word. 'Our ancient Minster contains two Parishes as you know. I am one of the St. John's Churchwardens but there are other unfortunate beings who belong to St. Martin's Parish. Clearly St. John's is pre-eminent because as the Church of St. John grew over the centuries, it overspread St. Martins until all that was left to show was a bit of old stonework and a few hapless Churchwardens. Therefore, I feel it behoves me to defend the Churchwardens of St. John's and their obviously superior position.'

'But Gilly that is absolutely no reason for arguing and fighting them. Surely you should all be on the same side,' I chided.

'Never in this world, St. Martin's Churchwardens are but a conglomeration of drunks and bullies. They write their own names in the prayer books which are actually meant for everyone and they become inebriated in the vestry every evening with their precious Rev. Coltman, who is quite the vilest of the vile.' Gilly maliciously took a pinch of snuff before sneezing theatrically into his brown tinged handkerchief.

I was appalled at his words. It's perplexing when you are on friendly terms with two people who absolutely loathe each other. Usually, it's best to say nowt for fear they'll quote you in their arguments. But while Reverend Coltman had God on his side, Gilly had his acid tongue which this time had really upset me, 'How can you say that about him? He's a lovely man, just look at what he's done for all the poor children, giving them teaching and apprenticeships and whatnot.'

Gilly just laughed at me, 'Ah, but what do you say about those poor old servants of his who have to pull that great weight along on his velocipede when he's too indolent to move it himself? Does your precious Reverend worry about their health and well-being? And when that blind man Charlie Mason bumped against him in the street, he was all for putting him in the Workhouse. No, you must face the essential truth that he spends his time just fretting over faraway slaves.'

Gilly would say anything to stir people up. I stood up with a rapidity that made him drag out his pocket watch to inquire how I could think of leaving at such an early hour. Ignoring him, I flung my tulle shawl over my shoulders and left without even begging the permission of Mr. Fox.

When he did eventually arrive back in Keldgate, I hastened to offer abject apologies for leaving without him, 'It was just because Mr. Sumner upset me and I dashed off without thinking.'

To my surprise Mr. Fox drew me to him and consoled, 'Nay lass you did the right thing. I know you mean well but you don't always judge well. He's an evil bastard. From now on, I don't wish you to have anything to do with him.'

I was quite taken aback at his words, 'Why, Mr. Fox, I know you don't agree with his politics and a lot of you Councillors get mithered with him for talking too much. But he's a very well-informed man. Look at that massive collection of antique books he has and all those ancient documents. He remembers absolutely everything he's read. No wonder he bamboozles those old Aldermen.'

'You don't know the half of what he's done, lass. Apart from smashing up the poor box and wine glasses in the Minster he causes fights, he publishes notices with all sorts of abuse about his fellow councillors, including my good self. But, of course he's too cowardly to put his name to his slander. He's been accused of buggery on several occasions. Of course, I wouldn't discuss things like that with a lady but seeing you aren't one, and you've probably heard much worse, I'll tell you straight, he's an evil bastard!' The wine Mr. Fox had taken loosened his tongue but then he abruptly released me from his embrace, turning rapidly to go out to the privy. He had begun to use it a lot more.

I knew Gilly quite well and although I was angry about what he said about Rev. Coltman, I couldn't believe all the other things said about him. Because he was always snooping about and asking impertinent questions, he'd soon worked out that Harriet was mine and Mr. Fox's. Years later he told me Mr. Fox should definitely have married me; Gilly had fallen out with his own father when he'd behaved in a similar way. It took Gillyatt Sumner senior five years to get round to marrying his second wife after she'd borne him a daughter; she was 29 years younger than him but obviously more persuasive than me. Seems unfair but what can you do?

Having a bairn came as a complete surprise to me. My monthly curses had always been unpredictable and at my age supposed I could have started on the 'change'. I'd shared Mr. Fox's bed so often that I'd come to assume I was barren. I assured him the baby was his but, of course, it could also have been fathered by any of the other three men to whom I'd been of service and, remember, Mr. Fox was over 70 years old. Although he directed most of my time, he was often away at meetings so I'd plenty of opportunities to secretly satisfy certain masculine appetites and get paid for it.

Now I beg you not to blame me for my promiscuity. I mean to say, even Rev. Joseph didn't blame me for my earlier liaison with his assistant curate. It was Rev. Robinson who was summarily dismissed because he should have known better, while I just received a long lecture after which I tearfully repented for my sin. My time as an actress was such an asset!

I had been forced into prostituting myself because of a casual dalliance I'd had in past years with William Denton who lived near us in Keldgate. This was not something I wanted to continue on my return to Beverley. Perhaps I was a trifle clumsy in the way I dashed his presumption that I would fall back into his arms. It was my mistake to intimate he was no longer the slim, handsome youth I remembered. He did then propose marriage but why would I wish to be tied to the type of man expecting his dinner on the table the minute he came home from his work before clearing off to spend his wages in the Spotted Cow? I needed to think of my future and realise my ambition of being in a position to escape menial tasks and order my own servants to take care of household chores.

William took rejection badly and malevolently told two of his friends about our past liaison. They came into the shop when I was alone, threatening to make trouble for me with Mr. Fox unless I met them at the back of Hinds Yard on a regular basis. For some months I made the most of this predicament as, knowing their wives, I could charge more than the regular 'nymphs of the pave'. Eventually I was saddled with my folly; Harriet was born in 1816.

The intermittent stomach pains I'd been suffering all day I put down to some boiled cod eaten the previous evening but it got progressively worse. I ended up screaming so loudly that Lucy Brownrigg from next door heard me through the thin walls and came rushing round to the house door. She'd had her own baby around a month before with her mother acting as midwife, so had a bit of an idea of what to do.

'Calm down Lizzie, you've got a baby coming that's all,' she soothed and got me to lie down on the kitchen floor while Mr. Fox made himself scarce. Not alarm myself! What else could I do but bite down hard on the side of my hand until it bled to stop screaming out loud?

'Head's there,' said Lucy, so matter of fact you'd have thought it was an everyday occurrence, 'Soon be over.' And so it was, after a convulsion of the most frightful character, two tremendous pushes and a weird slither, another human being entered the world. Lucy saw to all the other business while I shivered with the shock of what had just occurred. At thirty years old I became a mother.

It was terrifying to be left alone with a squalling baby. Lucy showed me how to get her latched on to my breasts then left me to go and suckle her own bairn next door. I was so pleased to open the door to her the following morning after a fraught and sleepless night. Mr. Fox and I had spent the dark hours deciding the best way forward. Once more I proposed that Mr. Fox should marry me to make everything regular. Again his excuses were endless. The time wasn't right, his work at the council was too important, his customers wouldn't like it.

'No,' he said, 'It will be best to say we'd found the baby on the doorstep, after all a taint upon a woman harms all connected to her.' Anyone would think a man had nothing to do with the production of a child.

Mr. Fox still paid me well and I had my bread and board so I had to acknowledge that his proposition to announce he was caring for a foundling was probably the best narrative we could come up with. To be fair I had few options, for given my spinsterish situation, what chance would I have of benefitting from the Lying-In Charity? I could even have ended up in the Workhouse or the Lunatic Asylum with the other unmarried mothers. Men had only to denounce you as being mad and there you'd end up. I heard about a woman in Wakefield who'd been giving music lessons to a vicar's daughter but when she asked for payment the miserly priest said she was insane and had her committed to the workhouse and there was not one thing she could do about it. However, while accepting I was saddled with my folly, I continued to add to my nest egg at the Bank.

To keep up our pretence of Harriet being an abandoned infant, there was no lying-in period for me. I was back in the shop, sitting when I could, discreetly attending to the changes to my body wrought by the unexpected birth. Lucy brought me some hartshorn from the apothecary because I was bleeding so much. She agreed to keep our secret to herself for a substantial settlement and she would also act as wet nurse, being very well-endowed in that department. I was sadly inadequate.

Luckily Lucy's own baby slept a lot, whether due to nature or laudanum I cannot tell you. Having read all there was to read about the rearing of babies, Mr. Fox was strict on allowing Harriet to imbibe nothing but breast milk for the first four months. I was then permitted to spoon-feed her but had to follow his instructions to the letter, being such a useless natural mother. Lucy guided me through everything else. She instilled in me the necessity of giving soiled napkins a rolling boil wash for a full half hour, which made me puke. She knew to lather a baby's bottom in lard to prevent soreness and when I became alarmed at seeing the child wracked by hiccups, Lucy laughed, saying it was a good sign, 'Hiccup and thrive, Lizzie, hiccup and thrive.'

It seemed generally accepted in the town that grocer and councillor, Mr. Richard Fox had adopted the little baby he'd discovered abandoned on his threshold. She would now be known as Harriet Fox. What a saint he was in the eyes of his female customers.

A curate was organised to officiate at the Baptism ceremony as Reverend Coltman was to be her godfather, thus ensuring he would always take a great interest in Harriet's welfare. I did confess to him that Harriet was mine and he made me recite a prayer of contrition almost as if I was a Catholic but I felt better for it. And also better for escaping from the clutches of my Hinds Yard clients threatening them with a Bastardy Order if they ever betrayed me to Mr. Fox.

To make everything look correct, I acted as Harriet's godmother and held the baby until her screaming and struggling compelled Lucy Brownrigg to take her from me. Being 'au fait' with the writings of Monsieur Rousseau, Mr. F. insisted Harriet should be allowed to kick freely and never swaddled.

It wasn't difficult to keep up our pretence. I believed even my parents didn't know she was mine. Although Harriet persisted in calling him 'Mr. Foxy', he was privately tickled at becoming a father when at his age, he really could have been a great-grandfather. I observed the fond smile on his face as he watched her play with her doll. He would pay for anything she needed, lovely toys, nice clothes, whatever was necessary.

Mr. Fox was a regular in the Reading Room coming back full of what he'd discovered from the books they had there. You'd go in the shop and find several feeble old women leaning on their sticks, nodding as if they understood what he was talking about, be it America or the planets. He was particularly keen to discuss some fellow named George Stephenson and his locomotive named Blucher which meant absolutely nothing to his audience.

I recall one particular evening when Mr. Fox had given me permission to join him in the parlour for glass of Madeira, almost like a married couple. The child was in her bed and I noticed Mr. Fox chuckling to himself

'Now what's tickling your fancy Mr. Fox?' I asked. I do find it irritating to be left out of a joke.

'It was my conversation with Reverend Coltman this afternoon. Even now I'm finding it remarkably amusing. You see for some reason we got talking about Italy and how it would be very interesting to visit there and see the sights. I'd been reading a book which had a description of the eruption of Vesuvius, that's a mountain that spews out boiling hot lava you see. It's called a volcano.'

'I do know that, I'm not completely uneducated,' I said.

'No, of course, of course, you're very well read for a woman,' he allowed. 'Anyway, there was the Vicar, astride his hobby horse outside the shop and I started telling him about the volcano erupting, causing devastation and the smoke and steam were still coming up out of the fissures for months after. But Rev. Joseph said "Like smoked haddock do you mean?"' Mr. Fox's shoulders were shaking with suppressed laughter.

'What on earth was he talking about I mused? It seemed such a strange thing to say. So I asked, "Forgive me your Reverence but I don't quite understand your allusion." And what he said was "Well I mean, do these Italians have smoked fish like our smoked haddock?"

'Then light dawned. My dear Sir, I said, I'm afraid you have the complete wrong end of the stick, I wasn't speaking of fish but cracks in the rock called fissures.' Rev. Coltman ignored the explanation, setting himself off back into town because he just fancied a nice big plateful of smoked haddock.

Chapter 9

How Mr. Henry Hunt became a National Hero

Motherhood was never easy for me. When Mr. Fox strictly forbade me to admit Harriet was my daughter, I was at a loss to know how I should behave toward her. I tried talking and singing to her, but was she interested? No. She wanted to play at shops just like her father. I dressed her nicely but she never did she like the same things as me. Whenever I struggled to get a brush through her corkscrew hair, she would scream the house down. As my lap was always repudiated in favour of anyone else, I came to realise it was pointless trying to ingratiate myself with her.

Sundays were when I regularly crossed over the road to have my Sunday dinner with Mam and Pa after morning service at the Minster. Sometimes Bill and Amy were there as well but on this particular day, when Harriet was about three years old, they'd walked across to Norwood to visit her brother. After all the usual cant, and before she'd brought anything to the table, Mother said to me, 'Why don't you bring that little lass of yours across with you next time?'

'Harriet do you mean?' I was startled. Why would Mam think she was mine?

'Don't you look like butter wouldn't melt, lady. That little lass is the spit of you at the same age, same gold curly hair and blue eyes. I'm damned sure she's yours but you certainly covered it up well, I'll give you that,' Mam said grimly, she'd obviously been bottling this up for some time. Pa, with his habitual indifference to me, just kept his eyes down on the table, arms folded.

'Why couldn't you tell us?' she kept on.

'Just thought it was easier for you not to know. But you really mustn't let on to anyone. Mr. Fox wouldn't like it to be known he had a bastard daughter. Not with his position on the Council.'

Surely my parents would know how Mr. Fox rather gloried in being a big fish in a small pond, the most successful grocer in Keldgate and a shining light in the Council Chamber. Why didn't they realise I hadn't admitted to having a child because I was shielding Mr. F. from his enemies on the Council? People like Mr. Nutchey who would seize any opportunity to accuse him of immorality and thereby destroy his precious reputation.

Alarmingly my mother's mouth opened wide in complete disbelief before screeching straight into my face, 'Mr. Fox is not the child's father. I will not believe it of him. But you, you've been carrying on with all sorts! You've no self- respect and we're both ashamed of you.' Pa shook his head and looked even more miserably down at his boots.

'Your wonderful Mr. Fox has been taking advantage of me since I was fifteen years of age if you really want to know the truth of it,' I protested, warm tears running down my cheeks. 'I knew you'd never believe me against him.'

I'd never been spoken to like this in my whole life. But such were my mother's prejudices against me, I would always be to blame; forever wrong and never wronged. 'If that were the case why would you go back and live over there again? You were welcome to lodge with our Bill and Amy.'

As Bill and Amy could do no wrong and had the expectation of producing a legitimate grandchild for them, there was no point looking for sympathy. Rashly I just came out with, 'It was you who told me to always do what Mr. Fox wanted.'

Mam's chair fell back on the floor as she launched forward at me only held back by Pa, who although spare was very strong.

'Just go, Elizabeth,' said Pa.

This wasn't my only problem. That morning, before I'd even got across to Mam's house, I was already on the verge of tears, upset by another raging altercation between Mr. Fox and me. This time, he was insisting on getting Harriet vaccinated with the cow pox to make sure she didn't catch the small pox. All the wealthy families were keen for their children to be treated with this preposterous innovation which Mr. Fox designated a 'miraculous experiment'. I had so little faith in the medical profession I was loth to give my permission but, as Mr. F. pointed out, I could have no part in the decision. In hindsight I can only wish that they could design similar inoculations for the dreaded whooping cough.

Mam, having successfully ruined my appetite, I arrived back at Mr. Fox's house in the lowest of spirits where I found him keen to continue our disagreement. What a memory he had for all my past failings. Our argument was made more complicated by the necessity of keeping our voices down so as not to alarm the neighbours or indeed Harriet. In a high-pitched whisper, Mr. Fox told me to pack a bag and leave. Nobody wanted me to remain in Beverley so the decision was easily made. I would pack a bag and turn my back on him, my disagreeable family and my mewling child.

Early the next morning, I awoke with a determination to visit Wiltshire. Well why not? Hadn't I always yearned to see Stonehenge from the very day Mr. Fox showed me an engraving of it? We'd spent a whole evening wondering at the ability of those human beings called Druids, who, thousands of years ago, had the skill to transport and erect such colossal monoliths. It was a strange ambition I know, but I possessed a strong urge to run my fingers over the same stones those ancient Celts had touched.

After a bite to eat, off I went to the Cross Keys to book a place with the booking clerk who suggested that my best plan would be to get to Hull for the London coach and enquire once I got there about the most convenient route to Wiltshire. Never before had he come across anyone who'd travelled there from Beverley.

The Golden Fleece at Beckside was where the coach to Hull set off. I'd enough money for inside; you'd never catch me clambering any old gimcrack ladder for an outside seat swept by wind and rain. Of course, if you go to York from Beverley, it's even worse for those up on top. They have to duck right down if they wish to keep their heads attached when going through that low brick archway of the North Bar.

I thanked the Lord that I was skinny and quick enough to get aboard first to secure the best seat, bag clutched tight to my chest. Stage coaches were a great wretchedness for anyone stiff in the joints and broad in the beam because they get wedged in and it's such a to-do every twenty miles or so for the change of horses when folk need to get down to stretch their legs or find a privy.

Coachie settled his buffalo robes round him, shouted 'All right? Ya Hip', blew his bugle and off we went. My low spirits faded and my shoulders relaxed. It was as if a weight had been lifted from my chest and once more I was able to breathe deeply.

Whenever the River Hull overtopped and flooded the area between Hull and Beverley, people and provisions could only transit on horseback for weeks on end. Therefore, the building of the turnpike had been essential for all the villages clinging to the firm ground among the bogs. Mr. Fox said, 'Just imagine fifty years ago, 4 ½ days it took to get from London to Manchester and now we've got turnpikes they get there in twenty-six hours. And there's no bother from them good-for-nothing highwaymen, they don't like paying the toll.'

When we got to Woodmansey we were stopped by the rope stretched across the road for the coachman to pay the toll. Next morning I was aboard the stage going from Kingston-upon Hull down to the Golden Cross Inn in London. This time I'd chosen to travel by way of Doncaster as I hadn't really enjoyed my last trip on the Steam Packet across the Humber. All that bobbing about made me nauseous for days afterwards.

After a few days there I was, back in dear old London Town. Roaming around on my own held no fears for me, knowing the place pretty well from my walks with Michael. I was advised to take a room at 'The Swan with Two Necks' in Cheapside in order to be ready for the early Exeter Coach which went via Salisbury, with a stop of just one night on the way. Journeys cost about 5d. a mile down south so I was careful to select the shortest route. Whenever the coach pulled up for a change of horses, you had to be quick to get out to the jakes and back on board so the coach didn't sally off without you but with your luggage. For twelve hours on and off, I sat in that coach.

You learn a lot, cramped up with people you may never wish to meet again. Men spit out their chewing baccy on the windward side and it comes back in through an open window. Anyone with beeswax or lard in their hair would find all manner of debris stuck in it. I was also put out of humour by fat people with stinking pies dropping crumbs everywhere. Thankfully on this journey, no one attempted shooting at wild beasts or birds; everyone should understand how that would scare the horses. Unfortunately, our horses found a different reason to bolt and my journey ended, quite unexpectedly, near a little village called Upavon.

A forceful young man on board had cajoled or bribed the coachman into letting him have a turn with the ribbons and set off, really waggoning it. His friend had grabbed hold of the coachman's horn, blowing it as loud as he could while the coachman yelled at everyone to sit still and hold tight. Needless to say, the horses set off at a gallop, couldn't negotiate a corner and scattered us all over the road, bags, bundles and all. The front of the coach was beat to pieces. Rapidly scrambling back to my feet, I grabbed the best bags I could carry. I'd rather not have met the fresh country air in such a precipitate manner but made the best of it by straggling along the road with some fellow who'd been keeping me well entertained on the coach and was familiar with the area.

On learning I was seeking work, he told me about a farmer in desperate need of a servant; he urged me to come along with him to Widdington Farm. The house he pointed out stood pretty well when compared with many dilapidated mansions we had already passed. I held no ambition to be a shepherdess but my new friend explained how this respectable gentleman, Mr. Hunt had told his neighbours he must find a housekeeper post haste. As we trudged my new friend explained more of the circumstances.

Henry Hunt's wife had debouched a few years back to live at her father's tavern and now he was in a fluctuating relationship with some woman; my fellow passenger called her his 'minx of a mistress'. After paying scores of men for the past several years to clear his land of noxious couch grass and weeds in order for his crops to thrive, at last Mr. H. could see his efforts rewarded with splendidly good harvests giving him more time to devote himself to his true passion, the Reform of the Great British Nation.

Those long French Wars had led to more and more land being cultivated here in England. Perversely as more grain was produced, the price dropped which of course brought about the contentious solution of the Corn Laws to keep imports out and our bread prices high; this resulted in greater rewards for farmers and yet more hunger and disappointment for the poor. Mr. Hunt stood out against the Corn Laws albeit they had allowed him to transform himself from farmer to reformer.

Without so much as a second thought, Mr. Henry Hunt welcomed me into his house, on the best wages I'd ever had. I gave my real name but said I'd spent some time as an actress in London. He was uncommonly handsome with hazel eyes set in a pleasing countenance. Even around the London theatres you would never see such a striking-looking gentleman. And what a talker! More of a gabster than even Mr. Fox and considerably more preoccupied with politics.

That first time I saw him is imprinted in my memory. Sporting a deep blue, lapelled coat and kerseys, his hair was thick and springy as a badger with a distinguished touch of grey at the temples. He was one of the tallest men I ever met apart that is from Mr. William Bradley from Market Weighton. Mam took me to see him when he visited Beverley because he was seven feet and nine inches high. But Mr Hunt was definitely the more handsome! His smile was disposed to expose almost perfect teeth, which I really like in a man. As soon as he came into a room, I would inhale deeply in order to relish his particular balmy pomade.

After his mistress absconded with a new beau, we got on more intimate terms. I would assist in vigorously rubbing his skin with his body cloth which resulted in his renowned healthy glow; he then would do the same for me. He was such a considerate lover, gallantly withdrawing, not wishing the encumbrance of children for which I was truly thankful. Although I will acknowledge I'd got over Harriet's birth quite easily when compared to the reported suffering of our poor Princess Charlotte.

There's a lot to be said for belonging to the bourgeoisie with our simple pleasures. Of an evening Mr. Hunt and I got into the way of sitting over a glass or two of Geneva in his snug wainscoted parlour, enjoying a bandying of words over a vast range of subjects. He liked to bring up philosophy as well as the woeful decisions of the government. We were at variance on the subject of William Wilberforce, a man I had always revered apart from his view that unmarried women should look no further for fulfilment than looking after the poor. Mr. H. derided his espousal of abolishing slavery while ignoring the plight of British workers. But after all, nobody's perfect.

'I'd like to hear your opinion of the actions of John Bellingham, Mr. Hunt?' said I one evening, wishing to see how the land lay.

'Of course, I can quite see his point of view; it was clearly our dishonest government who compelled him to go to such drastic lengths. For want of an honest House of Commons, John Bellingham must have been driven to despair. Manifestly their refusal of justice was the sole cause of that fatal catastrophe.'

'You comprehend the matter exactly, Sir. I worked for him in London and I can assure you he went to immeasurable lengths to get justice by presenting his petitions but absolutely no one there would listen to him,' I said.

'Did you really work for him? Well, I'm blessed. But violence should never be the answer, I will never condone that. I presume you had to seek another employer after he was hung or did you return to the theatre?' I was flattered to find how interested Mr. Hunt was in my life.

'No there was nothing suitable at the time so I found another housekeeping job with an agreeable gentleman,' I said, not wishing to name Mr. Holloway because of his connection with the Stock Exchange Hoax. Henry Hunt often railed against the aristocracy and particularly identified Lord Cochrane as being to blame along with everyone involved in the plot because their mendacity had callously deprived people of their hard-earned money. I shrugged off any responsibility myself for, as I told you, what I had done was patently an innocent misunderstanding.

Over the months Mr. Hunt and I had some rare old discussions about how to make the world a more equitable place. We discussed the Women's Union campaigning for their husband's political rights which I felt was ridiculous.

'Mr. Hunt,' said I, 'Surely women should be campaigning for their own rights. You must see it's quite monstrous for one half of the population to command such power over the other half.'

Mr. Hunt mischievously brought me down, again citing Mr. Wilberforce, 'Your hero takes the Biblical view that it is quite wrong for women to involve themselves in public affairs for they are vastly more moral than men and any move towards their emancipation would indubitably lead to an increase in female misbehaviour. And I would go further to say that any such campaign would inevitably retard the universal suffrage of men.'

Those few words informed me Mr. Wilberforce was not correct about everything and that women are not to be considered part of the universe.

The Manchester Patriotic Union sent a long letter to Mr. Hunt begging him to come to their city to address their members at a huge meeting. He passed it to me to read for, to my surprise, he had immediately decided to reject the invitation.

'But Mr. Hunt, you must do this.' I cried. 'It's what you are destined to do. Why in Heaven's name would you refuse your help to inspire people and bring about changes? I swear you will regret missing such a golden chance!'

'Calm down Elizabeth my dear. There is good reason for my hesitation I do assure you. I will agree the previous time I spoke in Manchester all was well organised and quite orderly. And it was the same last year in Spa Fields in London; I'd no trouble at all in getting a show of hands to elect me to take a petition to the Prince

Regent from the people of London. But after his High and Mightiness's downright refusal to see me, a second meeting was arranged and what a dreadful disaster that was! I arrived there ready to speak as before but before I could even get on to the platform, up jumped the notorious Mr. Arthur Thistlewood? Have you heard of him? Absolute madman! There he stood, Cap of Liberty on his head, tricolours waving around him, urging a huge drunken mob to march upon the Tower of London. No one on God's earth could have stopped them; absolutely hell bent they were on bringing about a British Revolution.'

'Oh, my word, I can just see how that would unsettle you,' I said. 'If that meeting was taking place in your name, you'd have been the one to blame if those addleheads were killed or put in jail.'

'Exactly right. Luckily the whole thing fizzled out but three of the leaders were arrested. Jolly fortunate they were to be acquitted of High Treason which I believe they truly deserved,' said Mr. H.

'That would never happen again, surely Mr. Hunt.'

'But if it did? What if another hothead like Thistlewood invaded the meeting? Do you believe I could countenance the deaths of innocent people if things got out of hand like that again? Now you tell me Elizabeth, if by any chance I do agree to go, just how can I reach out to those discontented people and find the right way of explaining the absolute necessity for universal suffrage and voting by ballot without risking rousing them to violence?'

I could see his difficulty; belonging to the landowning classes he obviously lacked my undoubted talent for fitting into every level of society. I made the most of being consulted on such an important matter. 'Now sir,' I said, 'you may recall me speaking of Michael Macready, my friend from my time at Drury Lane Theatre. Whenever he found himself down on his luck, he transformed himself into a field preacher. With his gift of the gab he could persuade even the poorest to part with money they could ill afford. Around the villages he'd go, painting the picture of the dire straits of crippled soldiers suffering the bloody horrors of the last war. Being an actor, he knew how to move a crowd emotionally.'

'Oh Lord, I know all that, stirring up is no problem to me,' said Mr. Hunt. 'Everyone agrees with my friend William Cobbett when he talks about the Government seeming to listen but never hearing, and seeming to look but having no sight. My difficulty is getting over to an angry mob the necessity of a planned course of action which does not involve a revolution or bloodshed.'

'I certainly would not wish you to follow Michael implicitly; he had no morals. But he could get folk to put a groat into his hat no matter how poor they were. And with a large enough crowd it provided him with a fair income. Wounded soldiers didn't benefit of course, but then they weren't expecting anything were they? And the crowd derived a smug feeling of doing a charitable deed.'

Mr. Hunt was looking puzzled so I went on, 'You must put on an act. Act sincere. Once you've got the crowd on your side, tell them the only way to get justice is for everyone to keep within the law. Together they may be strong but why give the military an excuse to fire on them or put them in gaol or pack them off to Botany Bay? Tell them that trumpets and pigeons were the only weapons employed by the audiences at the Royal Opera House and they got the ticket prices brought back down. Tell them Revolution is the way to lose, just look at France, they're back where they started, restoring their monarchy like that. People yearn for an honourable leader to depend on so make sure it's you and not Arthur Thistlewood.'

Mr. Hunt was undeniably correct to be worried about Mr. Thistlewood. You must have read of the frightful evening when the presumptive 'President of the Britannic Republic' and twelve of his supporters broke into a house where Members of the Cabinet were having dinner. Their intention was to chop off their heads and stick them on pikes for a parade through the London streets. The plot rebounded because the Bow Street Runners knew all about the conspiracy and were lying in wait for Thistlewood's men. Five of the conspirators were hanged and then beheaded themselves.

When the Manchester Patriotic Union arrived at the house in force to speak to him, Mr. Hunt demanded assurances from them that no violent Radicals would be allowed to speak. I was excluded from their discussion but I got the gist of their intentions, they wanted votes for more people and an end to famine and unemployment in the North as would any reasonable person. In good faith Mr. Hunt promised to attend and concurred with their stated hope of transferring the seat of real power from Downing Street and up to Manchester.

I'd never been to Manchester so decided to accompany Mr. Hunt in his gig. His so-called friend, William Cobbett castigated Henry for travelling about the country with a whore. But now I wonder why I should have given a fig about the views of that coward. He went around encouraging people to protest and then absconded to America leaving his followers to be imprisoned?

Mr. Hunt was only twelve years older than me and very handsome, better favoured in every way when compared to Foxy. We spent a pleasant night together in Stockport and the following morning outside our inn we found an open barouche adorned with blue and white flags waiting for us. Rather than a pair of horses, a group of strong men stood by until we were settled then gathered up the traces themselves to pull us along to St. Peter's Plain.

I was delighted to meet the Manchester Committee of Female Reformers; such visionary women were surely to be admired for taking a stance on their own accord. Sadly, with typical male depreciation Mr. Hunt ignored their ambitions and admired their white dresses which, he joked, was the reason he'd worn his white hat and white cord breeches to complement them. I too was wearing white in the hope it would help our soldier heroes coming back home from the war to no jobs and no pensions.

As we travelled along Deansgate followed by the ladies in white, people cheered and shouted for 'Orator Hunt', as Poet Robert Southey had dubbed him. Just like the Luddites and Blanketeers marching on London, Lancashire folk were prepared to do the same in Manchester; for days they solemnly practised marching up on the moors to show unity and determination.

They reckoned 200,000 people were gathered on that blazing hot day in St. Peter's Field, waving banners proclaiming 'Unity and Strength', 'Liberty and Fraternity' and 'Universal Suffrage' while a dozen bands played 'See the Conquering Hero Comes.' The standard which proclaimed 'Equal Representation or Death' caused uneasiness among the Yeomanry despite the crowd singing 'God Save the King' to indicate they intended no disrespect to the Royal Family.

Some folk who had walked for days to get to Manchester looked ready to drop. Despite the call going out for everyone to clean themselves up and wear their most decent clothes, the stench of the unwashed pressing around us in that heat was quite nauseating. Many sported red caps like those worn by the French Revolutionaries but all had been told to 'bring no weapon other than an approving conscience' although they were later accused of being armed. Everyone just wished for a Radical change or at the least to have more pleasure than pain in their lives.

Mr Hunt took my hand, helping me up on to the rully designated as his rostrum. We clung together tightly looking over that unbelievably huge mass of people gathering just to hear him speak. The festive atmosphere among the crowd persisted despite the Yeomanry positioning themselves around the edge of the Fields. The Free Trade Hall stands there now.

I'd managed to compose myself. My heart gradually settled down into its normal ebb and flow but as Mr. Hunt held me, I was alarmed to feel him trembling all over. It was then that I decided to let into him. Rather than allow any floundering at this point I put my own persuasive power into action.

'You want to actually do something for all those people, Mr. Hunt, just look at them, most have no work and those that have a job gave up a whole day's wage just to hear you speak. But think on, most have more interest in getting work than in getting a vote. Stand up there and show them you're not all mouth and white hat.'

His glance toward me told me he wasn't used to be spoken to like that, 'No one should ever doubt my courage, don't you worry,' he muttered. I kissed his cheek saying, 'Then off you go and show them you're on their side, turn your ripples into waves and shout as loud as you can. Remember, I'll have a special treat for you tonight.'

Looking down at his clenched fists for a few seconds before straightening out his fingers, he flashed his dimpled half grin toward me and nodded. I gave him a shove, 'Act your hat off Mr. Hunt and you'll get action. Be sincere, be on their side.'

Suddenly seized by a severe pain in the stomach I sensed an urgent need for a privy so slipped discreetly from the back of the rully. I could hear hundreds of voices cheering as Mr. Hunt stepped to the front of the platform waving his famous hat. Eyes almost popping from his head, he roared out his message while I made my way as rapidly as possible to the back of some houses on the edge of St. Peters Fields. Thankfully feeling better after managing to avail myself of the stinking facility, I found my way back guided by the noise from the crowd.

Some of the Manchester Troop of Yeomanry were lined up in front of the houses and, as I passed their Trumpeter, he signalled to me to pick up his instrument which had dropped from his sweaty grasp as he tried and failed to control his whickering horse. It charged heedlessly into the crowd before stopping, unable to move among the press of thousands of people. The Trumpeter's predicament apparently prompted all the 15th Hussars to enter the fray. Waterloo medals rattling, they sabred madly right and left, careless of whether men, women or children were knocked down. Amid the tumult I heard one fellow, desperately trying to protect his mother from a hussar's flashing blade, shouting, 'What are you doing? My Mam only came to see Mr. Hunt.'

Mr. Hunt's intention had been to avoid violence at all costs but once those Hussars charged forward things really got out of hand. Later they excused their action saying they moved in to rescue the 'stupid boobies' of the Manchester and Salford Yeomanry when they were surrounded by the menacing crowd. The excuse of the Yeomanry was that as local tradespeople wearing their 'regimentals,' they had the authority to control crowds in any way they felt necessary.

Some say the Magistrate was screaming for people to disperse, but who would have heard him? Organisers of the protest were yelling 'Standfast' and the Yeomanry, some stone drunk, were trying to prevent anyone leaving the area, creating yet more panic. Eighteen people were killed and over 400 injured on that dreadful day. Mr. Hunt was cut several times, twice through his hat. I watched as the soldiers dragged away some of the journalists along with Mr. Hunt. He shouted at me to get back to Widdington Farm to look after his dogs and not to forget to get the Parkers Rabies medicine for them. He loved his dogs.

The uninjured were rapidly disappearing into the maze of surrounding streets, evading the Militia as best they could. With my bonnet securely fixed back on my head, I picked my way carefully through the twitching bodies and motionless banners lying in the still, humid air. Past broken flag staffs, caps and shawls, I eventually found the barouche. Happily, I found our bags still stowed under the box seat but sadly had to leave Mr. Hunt's sweet little portable writing desk behind, being too unwieldy to carry. He took it everywhere to jot down his thoughts as they came to him; it would have been worth something.

You know we had rare old arguments at Widdington Farm on many matters. He usually wore me down with his superior erudition but I'm persuaded it was the precious time he spent discussing matters with me that made him the inspirational speaker he became. People used to call Mr. Hunt the 'best mob orator of the day' didn't they? But where do they suppose he got all his ideas from?

I can tell you it was definitely during those evenings spent chatting over our glasses of wine. I would describe the hard lives of those tannery workers I knew down Keldgate. The immense disjunction between them and the folk in the big houses meant nothing could ever change for them as the rich always voted their own sort into office. Who could expect the poor to always starve quietly? Why not give people a vote rather than drive them to violence? And surely any benevolent government should find work for all those poor lads coming back half daft from fighting the Frenchies.

Despite being a farmer, Mr. Hunt really meant it when he spoke about repealing the Corn Laws but he needed me to drum into him the absolute necessity of telling plain people plain truths. And speaking of corn reminds me of something else he should feel indebted to me for. I'm sure you'll remember that after those two years he spent in Gaol, he made his fortune from manufacturing his famous 'Breakfast Powder' that you drank instead of tea or coffee. Well, that was what I used to make every week with roasted corn to sell in Mr. Fox's shop. If ever there was a bag of grain at the back of the shop he wanted using up, he'd persuade me to find a way to make it palatable enough to sell. And whenever money was tight at Widdington Farm, I'd make the same thing for Henry Hunt. Of course, being a business man, he took my idea further and started up a proper factory anticipating that, because no tax was payable on such a drink, it would be worth his while to make my 'Breakfast Powder' for the masses.

When Henry Hunt got elected Member of Parliament for Preston, that's the one in Lancashire not East Yorkshire, lo and behold he did put in a petition for women to be allowed to vote just as I'd been telling him. He waved his finger at the Commons and they waved their Order Papers back at him. It brought about the best laugh ever in Parliament so they say.

I've never understood why there were people who hated Mr. Hunt. Some said he was a 'detestable monster', 'obnoxious, ill-informed but clever and resolute' and tried to ruin all his business efforts by publishing notices saying, 'thou shalt not buy Hunt's matchless blacking nor his ink nor his roasting grain nor anything that is his.' He was a Member of Parliament for only 3 years but at least he had a go at changing things so you had to admire him for that. Then he died.

Now let me get back to telling you about that day in Manchester. You can imagine how perturbed I was at seeing Mr. Hunt dragged off in such a brutal manner; I confess to being a little in love with him. However, you must understand, my own situation was also rather unpleasant. Stranded in a strange city where every one of my acquaintance had been imprisoned, who could I turn to? Mr. Hunt could no longer provide me with a home, protection or income. I could weep for him but not for those snide London journalists who having derided the ragged clothes of the rioters, became enraged at being arrested themselves. Our valiant Prince Regent actually congratulated those heroic soldiers for shooting at an unarmed crowd of men, women and children. Terrible lies were believed about that day.

It was only three o'clock and to me it seemed more judicious to return to Beverley rather than to Wiltshire, there being many more coaches travelling to Yorkshire. As for Mr. Hunt's animals, I trusted his estate manager would see to them. My responsibility was to myself and so I sought out a coach heading for Leeds and York. Its name, 'Trafalgar' commemorated Horatio Nelson's famous victory. In order to get a good seat, I bribed the driver with a poke of Church's Cough Drops and he helped me in with my bags.

The stops at Leeds and York might well have drained my purse but, fortuitously being left in sole charge of the 'Hunt Fighting Fund' I was delighted to find there was a great deal of spending left in it for me. Sad to report, I have yet to see Stonehenge.

Chapter 10

In Which the Case is Made in Favour of Bribery

Completely exhausted by previous day's events in Manchester, you can imagine how soundly I slept at the Bull and Mouth Hotel in Leeds. And I know you must be wondering whence it got its odd name, so I'll tell you. Due to years of mispronunciation, much as Michael Macready had pointed out long ago in connection to the Elephant and Castle in London, 'Boulogne Mouth' had referred to the Harbour at Boulogne in France which, in the patois of Leeds, had gradually lapsed into the 'Bull and Mouth.'

Having discarded my grubby white Reformist gown at said hostelry, I travelled in my dark green silk with matching braiding. On stepping from the coach in Beverley, I engaged an urchin to carry my bags. On our way through Wednesday Market Place back to Mam's house in Keldgate, I couldn't help noting various aspects of the town had changed in my absence. Before they actually fell down, several hovels had been carefully demolished to ensure their tiles and wood could be incorporated into the many smart new mansions; canny builders viewed it as a good way to keep down costs and so increase their profits. As I constantly assure you, there's not much goes to waste in Beverley!

Vaguely familiar figures gave me a quick glance as they strolled by, saying nothing. To be quite honest such dowdy people were of no interest to me. Having grown into my own person while I'd been away, I felt my priority was to devise some sensible connected plans to improve my future. Should I stay or should I go? Should I look for somewhere to rent for myself or would it be advantageous to move back in with Mam and Pa? I was certain Mam would not consider evicting any of her settled tenants for my sake.

The Taylor family were what some might call the 'middling sort.' My parents had several properties rented out; they never wished to become beholden to anyone. There was little hope for me to be anything but 'Middle' either. You can only break into the Upper Class through marriage and for me that was supremely unlikely. As the poet said, the Upper Class had 'hearts of oak' whereas the Middles were merely 'veneered'. However, if a Revolution ever does become a real danger here, there's a lot to be said for being Middle; it has always been the Middling Sort that wrought change. Uppers couldn't maintain the status quo without them and Lowers couldn't achieve a change in governance without the education and enfranchisement possessed by the Middles.

It turned out I needn't have considered the risk of causing more domestic dissension by moving back home. Bill and his tedious Amy were living at Mam's house so there was no room for me anyway. We grudgingly agreed a truce, promising to forget the rancour of our last parting and let by-blows be bygones. As they were soon to become legitimate grandparents for the first time, my parents magnanimously deigned to overlook Harriet.

Clearly in the history of the world no one had suffered a pregnancy like Amy's. Mam tutted and grumbled behind her back while Pa just pottered out in his workshop until it was dark. He preferred the damp cold to the stuffy fug of the parlour where shuttered windows and thick curtains excluded any hint of draughts.

It was Bill who suffered most, having to find time after working all day to rub his wife's back and feet and anything else she proffered as well as providing treats she fancied. But he never complained. He was excited at the thought of becoming a father. When lads on Keldgate used to yell 'Willie Taylor?' others would shout 'Will he hell', insinuating he was impotent. He'd always suffered badly from teasing because of his size, his stammer and his name. Being a slow scholar, he'd been kept down in a lower form for two years so he looked like Gulliver in Lilliput amongst the younger children until one day he point-blank refused to attend school. Pa believed Bill learned more from him than any schoolmaster could instil.

Now that Bill could show the neighbourhood that he was capable of fathering a child he willingly indulged Amy's variety of whims. It proved expensive for, in the larder, along with other extra provisions, were oatmeal, allspice, beer and gin for the caudle she considered essential to revive her after the anticipated ordeal of confinement. I'd missed so much by concealing Harriet's birth, particularly all that gin for the painful contractions. Much of the stored goods unaccountably disappeared on a regular basis; Amy was twice the size of the woman I remembered.

No, I could never have borne the dissonance at Mam's house. So, once again, I accepted the humblest of pies and moved in with Mr. Fox and my daughter. He'd aged markedly since I'd last seen him. While not actually stooping, he inclined forward like a fence post after a cow had leant into it. There was no raking of old ashes, the spark had gone but he appeared quite relieved to see me. Quite curiously he grasped both my hands saying, 'At last you've come back where you belong.'

He was getting a bit forgetful and as his accounts were in a bit of a mess as well as the shop, I spent time sorting his bookkeeping, altering his spelling to agree with modern usage. It was as if my absence had never happened. To get the place more appealing to our customers I found it came naturally to me to issue orders to the new girl who obeyed me with a gratifyingly wholesome fear after the severe scolding I gave her for breaking lumps off the loaf sugar. She sorted the shop's shelves as I polished the windows gin bright, brushed down the curtains, scuttled out spiders, courageously disregarding the unpleasant feeling of crisped dead moths or sticky cobwebs wrapping my fingers in uncharted corners.

After a bit of a fall in Cross Street Mr. Fox felt more foot-sure if he held on to me while going about his business in the town. His disinclination to own a carriage stemmed from him liking the facility of roaming the streets as a man of the people, hailing acquaintances, slapping backs and shaking hands. It was not merely for the sake of common gossip he said, but it was important for Councillors to be aware of what was really important to their town. How else would they have known that the lower classes would prefer typhus and cholera epidemics rather than the rates going up for improvements to the water supply and sanitation which the Government had decreed was necessary? The Council did order the repair of some wells and pumps, starting with the one outside Mr. Fox's shop, naturally.

As we walked around the streets, by pressure on my shoulder Mr. Fox steered me toward people he wished to accost. His need to control and cocoon me had changed not a jot. He was forever reproaching me with having left him with Harriet, conveniently forgetting he'd told me to pack my bags.

Harriet didn't remember me with any great pleasure and I must say I didn't encourage her. A nursemaid now lived in as her substitute mother instead of Lucy Brownrigg; she'd borne another child during the time I'd been away. Harriet liked to play with her dolls and every evening Mr. Fox would sit her on his knee and read to her, thrilled when she pointed out words to him. She must have got her fancy for reading from him because she never would look at books with me. They played games together, making words with a set of bone counters etched with the letters of the alphabet.

As I concentrated on the business of getting the shop shipshape, Mr. Fox became even more involved in his beloved Council work. A boy was hired for the heavy lifting in the shop and to walk him down to the Guild Hall so he could concentrate on arguing and pontificating at his endless meetings. He was a Tory who preferred the old ways, sneering at the new money brought in by industrialists and professional people. I thought to impress him by telling of the long chat I'd had in Hyde Park with Mr. George Canning, but he dismissed this as one of my fancies.

Please don't think I'm complaining about my situation. Perhaps there was a little less drama here than in London or Manchester but when election time came around in Beverley you would find excitement aplenty among the freemen born in Beverley. I'd been raised in a Whig household but what really mattered to Mr. Fox was his claim to a slight familial connection to the newest Tory candidate. Although Richard Fox's two nephews lived in Beverley, he had little to do with them, whereas he felt having a hand in getting Mr. George Lane Fox elected would definitely increase his power and influence in the town. He even looked into acquiring his own coat of arms in the style of the Lane Foxes. It worked both ways as George Lane Fox felt it would give him more clout to be able to claim a local connection.

With impassive eyes he watched his agent blithely handed over bags of coins kindly prepared by the banks for Mr. Fox's plumpers' box. Voters preferred Honest-to-God sovereigns rather than copper tokens to help them decide where to mark their cross therefore all candidates accepted the inevitability of very large debts by the end of every campaign. Whigs and Tories have always agreed between themselves to overlook the others' so-called 'malpractices'; they both operated in similar ways. Among their myriad ploys to influence the voters, as well as handing out hundreds of sovereigns, they paid 'rent' for rooms never used or rewarded any freeman for checking the Minster clock whether or not he knew how to tell the time.

Bribery, now being denounced as blameworthy, has gone on for years; freemen drank in the system with their mothers' milk. Over fifty years ago, even my blessed Mr. Richard Sheridan was in trouble for paying the burgesses of Stafford five guineas each to get their vote. No one bothered and money spread helpfully around the town. As I'm sure you know, Mr. Bethell out at Rise Park, like many country gentlemen, finds it in his interest to look after his estate workers so gives them food and blankets and, in return, they keep him at Westminster.

For days before the election, excitement and interest was stirred up with processions a-plenty; banners waved and bands entertained the crowds, all financed by the candidates. I was commanded to organise some lads down Keldgate to act as messengers or give out flags and rosettes in party colours to anyone prepared to wear them around the polling booths. I saw Lucy Brownrigg trundling around Saturday Market with a huge feather in her cap, like a flag on a mud-ship.

Innkeepers all wished polling lasted longer than just the one day because candidates happily footed all the bills. However it wasn't just 'tavern influence' that made a difference to polling figures. At a house down Vicar Lane I was commissioned to pour 'tea' for tipsy potential Liberal voters who had accepted too much free ale. Helpful Tory supporters brought them along, promising a nice cup of tea to sober them up. A woman such as myself, blessed with the invisibility of middle age, even with a dead chicken on her head, would never be noticed adding a large pinch of laudanum to the brew causing the Whig vote to shrivel.   Sometimes feminine deficiencies can be turned to advantages.

Although Tories' usual colour was blue, in Beverley for whatever reason, crimson was favoured.   A stuffed fox, decorated with crimson feathers was carried on high along Toll Gavel to the sound of clashing pans and kettles. As Mr. Richard Fox and I were invited to attend so many party dinners and breakfasts, I'd had a particularly fine crimson dress made, courtesy of Mr. George Lane Fox.

Having the soubriquet 'The Gambler', George Lane Fox was well-known for losing money. Although, to be fair to the man, his name was at the top of the list of donors when he gave £52.10s for the Benefit of the Poor. But it must have been my tea that helped him get 1,038 votes out of the 1,278 polled for the man was an absolute buffoon. Albeit with such lavish bribery to rely on, what need had he to impress with words of wisdom?

You should have heard the good laugh he got when he stood up on the hustings for half an hour, burbling and stammering. Mistakenly convinced he was still a 'neck or nothing' young blood, he had dressed quite unsuitably for a hot day in a market town.   His monogrammed kerchief constantly hovered to stem the sweat streaming down his face while his stomach strained at the buttons of his fashionable waistcoat.   Mr. Richard Fox had to give him a good talking to before he could even get him onto the platform, telling him what to say and then doing his best to rally the crowd by enthusiastically stamping and cheering.   After such exertions I had to bear the weight of him for ten minutes while he caught his breath.

After the proclamation of the results, Lane Fox was chaired around the Market Cross.   In the course of his journey his silk hat disappeared and there was a real danger of him spewing all over those carrying him.   Once he'd staggered from the chair, the lads took it to the front of the Kings Head to smash it to smithereens. His triumph complete, Mr. Lane Fox thanked me for my efforts which, he stressed, had made all the difference to the result and presented me with a sweet little silver vinaigrette. I'm pretty certain

I still have it in a drawer somewhere among a tangle of brooches and laces; perhaps I'll bequeath it to my niece Amelia.

Contemplating Mr. Lane Fox up there on the hustings acknowledging the clamorous roars of the crowd, that dreadful day back in Manchester leached back unbidden into my mind. I've bought a coloured print of it from Mr. Kemp's shop at yon end of Saturday Market, because it actually depicts me up on the rully with Mr. Hunt, sunning myself in the delight of the moment. The artist has caught exactly the crush of people in the foreground and there am I, portrayed bold as you like in my white dress, holding a standard with 'Let us die like men and not be sold like slaves'. Beside me Mr. Hunt, the only man with a white hat, takes central position. His musky pomade haunts me still. There was a man who exuded charm, so sadly lacking in George Lane Fox.

And after all that effort and expense, did we see our chosen Member again and did he speak up for the town in Parliament? To the very best of my knowledge, no, not ever.

Of course, nothing as shocking as what they are now calling 'The Peterloo Massacre' could ever be contemplated occurring here in conventional Beverley. But, let me tell you, we did once come perilously close to it after the 'Great Football Match' between men from the villages and men from the town. Bob Spence took a vicious kick at the ball causing it to soar clean over the top of the North Bar from the corner of York Road prompting a huge cheer from the crowd who surged through the archway into North Bar Within. Unfortunately, they collided violently with the Mayor and his corporation, simultaneously emerging from a service in St. Mary's church. The indignity of being knocked off his feet so incensed the Mayor that, in revenge, he actually banished football from Beverley forever.

So much was going on in 1823 that, looking back now, I'm unsure of the order in which things occurred. I know Mr. Hunt got out of prison and wrote his memoirs, thankfully without any mention of me. And here in Beverley there was that scandal of the Mayor being involved in a paternity suit which Mr. Fox conspicuously avoided discussing, claiming his time must be devoted to examining a wonderfully erudite book on the 'History and Antiquities of the

Town of Beverley'. The author, our local historian Mr. Poulson had asked both him and Rev. Coltman to examine the text for inaccuracies and make recommendations before it went off to the printers. Every minute Mr. F. was at home he spent hunched over the manuscript, spectacles nipping his nose, gratified to think that his opinion was so valued. I was forever soaking bits of flannel with elderflowers boiled in milk to soothe his sore eyes. Then he died.

Mr. Fox was 78 years of age when he dropped dead in the Guild Hall 'in discharge of his duties' as a Magistrate. This is recorded on his marble plaque in the Minster but, as everyone knows, all plaques omit any unsavoury aspects of a life. Just take a look at mine on my Alms Houses if you don't believe me. Those with him when he died said he looked sprack and ready to chide everyone for making a fuss as he lay there clutching his pipe; the hot ash left a mark on the floor. He's still there, so they say, haunting the Guild Hall, stomping around on Council business. I've definitely caught a whiff of his favourite tobacco near the back staircase.

It was around that same time that Queen Caroline turned up at Westminster Abbey ready to be declared Queen at her husband's Coronation but the door was slammed in her face. Three weeks later she died; King George IV declined to attend his own wife's funeral.

For Mr. Fox's funeral, his two nephews pointedly excluded me from any of the arrangements. As next of kin, they clearly expected to be the sole beneficiaries despite them never coming near nor by. When Mr. Matthew Empson, the solicitor, read the will to those assembled in the parlour it was quite amusing to witness their woeful disappointment on hearing the bulk of Mr. Fox's estate was bequeathed to his 'dear daughter Harriet'. The nephews stared at each other, round-eyed and mouths agape, closing by degrees as they learned their substantial annuities were of a similar size to my own. Stoically holding back on recriminations or any attempt to exchange words, they allowed themselves a slight bow toward me and Mr. Empson and left in grim silence.

Chapter 11

Miss Harriet Fox Widens Her Horizons

Now the shop had become Harriet's property, it was of course my maternal duty to take charge of running it for her, still without disclosing that I was in fact her mother. Labouring more diligently now than I ever had for Mr. Fox, I controlled every aspect of the business but continued to neglect other maternal duties by paying the nursemaid to continue looking after my daughter's everyday needs. They even worked together stitching a sampler, such a useless employment as I've always supposed but I dutifully praised it, had it framed and hung in the parlour behind the door.

To my dismay Harriet came to blame me for her father's death. In her eyes I'd been neglectful in not realising he was forgetting to eat or drink while working so hard. Any rebuttals I gave her were abruptly rejected and she made such a dust about any changes I tried to make in the house or the shop, it quite brought me down. Thankfully, after what seemed like months of miserable bickering, my dependable advisor, Reverend Coltman, took me aside and suggested we ask his cousin to recommend a suitable family to take over the care of Harriet in order to equip her to enter society.

I seized upon the idea immediately, absolutely convinced this was exactly what Mr. Fox would have wished for his daughter. As you know he'd always fostered great admiration for the lifestyle of the gentry who regard it as normal to send their children away to be educated. And obviously, with no experience of being a lady myself, how could I prepare my daughter for a successful life and an ability to cope with her inheritance? With dispatch everything was arranged. Harriet would travel with Mr. William Coltman and his wife to stay with their friends, Mr. and Mrs. Brooke of Garmston in Shropshire who had two daughters, a little older than Harriet. I have no notion of anything being said about my particular interest in the matter.

The idea of travelling to a different part of the country and meeting new friends appeared to please Harriet. We invested some of her money in the purchase of new clothes, shoes and a travelling bag. Her grandmother gave her a beautiful little workbox with reels of silks, a measure and a housewife of needles so she could make her own pinafores and so on. Mam had found it at the back of a cupboard in one of the cottages they'd bought to rent out.

Before setting off on her great adventure, Rev. Coltman took Harriet aside and impressed upon her that she should write regularly, telling him every detail of her days. Without her knowledge, he promised to share all her letters with me. As the stress of rearing a disputatious child ebbed, I began to nurture some smug satisfaction for being a responsible mother doing the very best for her daughter. In Beverley most people didn't think well of those who gave up their children. But she wasn't mine, was she?

After the turbulence of the past few years, I found myself quite content to be free of coach travel and unsavoury tavern bedrooms not big enough to whirl a kitten round. Now I could just allow my life to drift along soberly and serenely as the ostensible proprietor of Fox's Grocery store with no one to tell me different. However, quite out of the blue one morning I received a note from Rev. Coltman asking me to visit him for a dish of tea at my earliest convenience.

I knew I hadn't been summoned merely to discuss a letter from Harriet, because our usual arrangement was for a boy to be sent to let me know when one had arrived and I would stroll down to the Vicarage later in the day after locking up the shop. Mystified, I hastily called in Lucy Brownrigg to take over behind the counter, removed my pinafore and bustled down to the Vicarage.

Some boys from the Bluecoat School were there for a lesson. In their neat blue coats with yellow collars and gilt buttons they remained silently reading their Bibles in the library while the Vicar and I sat down to tea and scones in his parlour. After exchanging commonplace news of our recent lives, the Reverend gentleman cleared his throat saying he wished to have a serious word with me about Harriet.

Smoothing his hands over his vast belly he said, 'Pray do not look so worried my dear Elizabeth, I merely wish to discuss a matter with you in view of our position as joint godparents. Harriet is doing very well but I'm sure you must agree with me that she is coming to an age when she will no doubt begin to ask questions about her parentage.'

The fact that no such thought had ever crossed into my mind quite startled me. 'Do you really believe so? I thought we had explained it all to everyone's satisfaction, we weren't really shamming.'

'Now as a God-fearing man you know I must insist that honesty is the best policy in all things. And whilst in prayer last night it suddenly came to me that now is the very time to set things straight. You will surely agree with me on this Elizabeth.'

I nodded mutely whilst thinking the exact opposite. Did I wish to put things straight? Is it truly dishonest just to avoid telling the whole truth?

'So, this is what I propose. As you know, my cousin William and his wife are on very good terms with Mr. and Mrs. Brooke so see quite a lot of our dear little girl. I was thinking I could direct them to find an opportune time to take Harriet aside to have a private word. They could explain that you are indeed her true mother who loves her and thinks of her constantly but only wishes her to have the best possible start in life. Sadly, they could say, Mr. Fox forbade you to claim to be her mother for fear of damaging your reputation in the town. There, that should exonerate you and enable you to build a proper relationship with your daughter. What think you?'

I mulled for a time before speaking, 'I suppose if you and your cousin both believe this to be the best way forward, then I must agree. What a strange thing it will be to suddenly become the mother of a ten-year old daughter. I don't know how well it will go down in Beverley.'

'I can assure you there are not many around here who don't already suspect you of being Harriet's birth mother, my dear. All your family came to work things out and you know how your dear sister-in-law delights in scandalmongering.' I gave a wry smile for I knew how much Reverend Coltman also loved a gossip although I do not believe he ever told people about the time he found me in 'flagrante delicto' In the Vestry with his curate.

The Vicar summoned his man to help him attain a standing position from which to bid me farewell and urged me to write to Harriet within two weeks, 'with all the eloquence of which you are mistress.' Myriad attempts at writing this particularly difficult letter to Harriet lay screwed up on the parlour floor before I found any eloquence whatsoever. I clung to our arranged story while emphasising how much I regretted misleading her, saying the fabrication was done for the best of reasons. Imagine my joy when she replied to my letter in the September of 1826:

'My Dear Mother, thank you for your letter. I was very pleased to find I do have a mother. I am sorry I did not write sooner. I am quite well, indeed I have not had a day's illness since I came to Garmston, excepting the measles. I am now quite well and happy, your affectionate daughter, Harriet Fox.'

You cannot imagine the delirium of joy that swept over me on receiving what must be the shortest letter in the world. I still have it safely stored in Mr. Welburn's Davenport desk.

Chapter 12

Election of the Whig Member for Beverley

That unforeseen surge of maternal love did not last long I'm afraid and soon I lazily lapsed into my normal state of selfishness. I did not wish to rush things and confess it was actually several years before I did get around to making the effort to confront Harriet in person as her true mother. My pathetic excuse to myself was that I needed to improve the shop and assiduously engaged in learning about accounting and ordering and so forth.

I often sought business advice from one of my cousins, Robert Taylor, self-satisfied owner of the grandest grocery emporium in Saturday Market. On inheriting it from his father he'd brought about all sorts of innovations with a view to providing his family with a respectable income. Late one afternoon he turned up in Keldgate as I was desultorily tidying the shop and sweeping the floor. I saw him peer through the window, then quickly looked up and down the street before coming in.

'Now then cousin Elizabeth,' he began. He was a big man for a Taylor, a bit like our Bill in his manner.

'Good afternoon sir, have you come to see how to run a successful grocers' shop?' I bobbed at him.

'Nay lass it a bit too quiet down here for me. You should be in the town centre, that's where you get the crowds.' Looking through the window and seeing nobody he smoothed down his hay- coloured whiskers before showed his yellowing teeth in what I took to be a smile.

'This does me fine, thank you. Wouldn't want to put you out of business by moving nearby.' I was carefully shaping my words in the Beverley way. Robert never liked anyone to get above their station. He said, 'How do you feel about earning a bit extra? You've no Richard Fox to rely on now have you? Wouldn't like to see you go short.'

Robert never had much time for Mr. Fox with him being a Tory. He preferred to meet up with local, forward-thinking Whigs like that George Leeman in York who has been all for investing in the new railway companies; they guarantee to bring prosperity to every town and city building a railway station.

'Go on then, what would I have to do?' I deemed it prudent to keep Robert unaware of my annuity from Mr. Fox and my satisfactory bank balance otherwise he may not think it necessary to pay anything for my help.

'Bit like what you did when that George Lane Fox got elected, but this time it would be to help us Whigs. You don't have to pretend you're a Tory any more now Fox has shuffled off his mortal coil, God rest him.' Robert assumed an unconvincingly doleful face.

'Yes I know, and I'm all for the Whigs but your John Wharton did really badly before. He used to be always top of the poll but last time there he was, right down at the bottom.'

He knew I was right. 'Aye I know love, but now Wharton's given up. Can't afford it any more. But we've got a damned good fellow, Mr. Daniel Sykes standing with Henry Burton.'

'Not one of those Sykes from Sledmere is he? You know they've no common sense.' And I told him Pa's story about Sir Masterman and his Boney bet. Even now, at his advanced age, his brother, Tatton Sykes, refuses to get on a railway train and insists on riding all the way down to London on horseback.

'Well I think there is some connection, cousin or summat. But this Mr. Daniel Sykes, he's a different kettle, your Pa would've backed him I haven't a doubt. Speaks out against slavery and bribery in elections. Although we'll have to keep that last bit quiet.' Robert's eyes looked amused while his mouth did not. 'It was him set up the 'Rockingham & Hull Weekly Advertiser', and you read that I do know. He's not one of your usual worthies taking their turn for a seat. Just up your ginnel he is. Come on lass, help us out.'

I could see Robert was in earnest and now being a woman of property, I did take more of an interest in our local politics. Obligingly I promised to go to Whig headquarters to set down on a slate the names of all those pledging their vote to the Whigs. Robert had obviously noticed my meticulous handwriting on the boards outside the shop and comprehended the lack of reading and writing skills among his political friends. The poll book always had to be carefully checked later to ensure those who had taken their customary payment had been men of their word, thus allowing their names to be wiped from the slate.

Local business men and landowners engage agents, such as our Robert, and get them to offer jobs or money to anyone with a vote who promises to put their cross in the right place. Men in possession of two votes would choose to use one for a sovereign and the other for a principle. Naturally, because of our Robert being a grocer, everyone called Whig bribes 'Beverley Sugar.'

Shopkeepers such as my Mr. Fox always knew the freemen worth taking aside for meaningful discussions about the myriad benefits available to those voting for Tory candidates. For instance, Mr. Fox would have known it would be totally unproductive to discuss Tory politics with my father. Landed gentry supplying most Tory candidates have a different set of priorities to the professional classes. Most never thought of actually meeting their constituents, election agents did that and promised, on their behalf, to sort any particular grievances. Despite a law against employees voting for their own employer it is disregarded. For several years now, Henry Edwards has made sure of always getting voted in because he bought the Iron Works along with its workforce.

When I met Mr. Daniel Sykes I knew he was the kind of candidate I'd be proud to oblige. He didn't pay voting money, just the expenses of anyone forced to travel up from London. In the House of Commons he led a plea for reducing taxes, an obvious and sensible help for small businesses like mine. Similar to Mr. Hunt, it was the true backbone of the country Daniel Sykes wished to represent – the workers. Tragically he succumbed to a cancer only two years after being elected.

Perhaps you cannot condone bribery, but you must understand why anyone blessed with a vote would try to get the most from it. There's folk down Keldgate who relied on elections to support their families, waving their voting paper about, asking to be 'persuaded.' Those fools accepting tickets for 10 free pints of ale at the Angel or the Tiger and ended up insensible and robbed or drowned in the Beck obviously didn't make the most of the largesse on offer. And those who accepted free cups of tea in Vicar Lane could lose a day of their lives and their chance to vote.

Everything is all sorted now though after those Bribery Commissioners came to Beverley to put things straight. Although both Whigs and Tories have always manipulated voters in exactly the same way, who do you suppose attracted most blame? Why the Whigs of course. Tight-fisted tradesmen and business people wouldn't part with any of their brass to engage expensive lawyers like the Tories do.

Only a couple of years ago Daniel Boyes, landlord of the Angel and our Robert were ordered to appear before the House of Commons committee in London inquiring into their part in offering bribes in the 1859 election. Well past midnight and carrying torches, hundreds turned out to greet our returning local heroes at Beverley railway station. The Beverley newspapers reported 'females in a half-dressed state joined the crowd as it passed their houses.' Before you ask, I was not one of them!

Daniel Boyes gave not a monkey's curse about the accusations made against him. So full of himself was the 'Prime Minister of Beverley' he stood outside the Angel Inn grinning and shouting to the crowd, 'I am not sorry the prosecution has fallen upon me. It might have fallen upon someone with a more nervous temperament.'

He wasn't laughing last year though, was he? He was found guilty at York Castle in 'nine several cases.' More than a hundred people were found to have accepted bribes an under-estimation I've no doubt. But I must ask you, why should the authorities suddenly decide to blame my cousin Robert and Daniel Boyes for a tradition that had been followed by all parties for generations? They were our local heroes.

Sorry for my rant, but I did say I was determined to get everything off my chest.

Chapter 13

London Diversions

So away with our dismal talk of politics and bribery! My daughter had now assumed more importance in my life. As our correspondence became ever more regular, I learned news of all the delightful things she was getting up to. Her letters always began 'Dear Mother' however when we did eventually meet, I was politely addressed as 'Mama' as I believe is comme il faut among the upper classes.

Now, as you know, I never have believed it to be improper to seek beyond your given station in life for where would we be if everyone remained in the same situation for perpetuity? I was gratified to learn that Harriet's proxy parents, Mr. and Mrs Brooke, were particularly well-connected; close acquaintances of the Duke and Duchess of Carlisle and their influential circle no less.

You can imagine the delight I felt on receiving the news that my dearest Harriet had the opportunity of staying at Chatsworth House in Derbyshire to recuperate after her nasty spell of the measles. She wrote to me of the kindness the Duke of Devonshire himself had shown by presenting her with two baby hares which, for some reason, she named Tiny and Puss. Her next letter nonchalantly informed me of their death within a matter of two weeks. The dear girl took everything in her stride.

With Mrs. Brooke and her daughters, Harriet visited several of the towns along the English south coast, becoming particularly fond of the sea-bathing towns of Brighton and St. Leonards-on-Sea where the girls acquired a passion for collecting shells and pebbles. When Mr. and Mrs. Brooke eventually took a house at Bromley, near to London, Harriet began to attend a school for young ladies run by the Misses Shepherd who arranged educational trips for their girls.

Harriet's absence from Beverley ushered in a closer association between me and the Rev. Coltman. A regular highlight of my week, was when Harriet's letter arrived addressed to either of us, we got into the habit of sharing and discussing her news over tea and cakes in his brimming library. He was constantly adding to his collection of rare tomes. As he looks down from heaven, he must find it gratifying that his passion for books has resulted in a library in Kingston-upon-Hull becoming the fortunate recipient of over two thousand of his precious books.

'I do so enjoy our little tête-à-têtes, Elizabeth,' he would say. 'You cannot conceive how isolated I feel in the Vicarage sometimes you know. Most of my visitors usually come here imploring for help or advice and then leave me to worry over them. My servants are very good but of course, they have their own tasks to get on with; no time for conversation.'

I hid a wry smile as I recalled how exasperated Pa had been years ago while trying to get on with widening the Vicarage doorways and the Vicar constantly detaining him for chats.

'Mrs. Atkin is a wonderful cook but you know, I must be so careful for whenever I praise a particular dish, I do seem to get it over and over again. And she knows how much I love my puddings. Spotted Dick, Bread and Butter,' he sighed. 'And she does make a beautiful Queen of Puddings. She has mentioned in passing that she expects some to be left for the following day but I know it would upset her if I didn't eat it all.' As usual, the Vicar's cheeks quivered as he chuckled.

Oft times I would urge him to try and cut down on what he ate because with his great weight; he had such trouble getting around his parishioners. His reply was, 'The truth is Elizabeth, I really eat very little; but in actual fact being overweight runs in our family. My sister is exactly the same. But you know I'm still nowhere near the size of Mr. Daniel Lambert; he was 53 stones. Now that is really heavy.'

Before I could ask the chicken and egg question, 'Do you get fat because you walk so slowly or do you walk slowly because you are fat?' he said, 'Now let us turn the conversation to our dear Harriet.

You must share my delight at her getting the benefit of all these splendid experiences she writes about.'

'Oh of course I do. And it is all absolutely due to your foresight and your cousin's splendid connections, thank you so much, Sir. I shudder to think what would have become of the two of us had she stayed with me in our miserable state of perpetual disagreement.' I smiled fondly at him.

I had to be honest, Harriet and I had never seen eye to eye. Now she seemed to have discovered contentment with her bosom friends, Isabella and Eugenia Brooke. Through her letters I was delighted to discover she had inherited my love of the theatre though not my facility with punctuation, having total inattention to full stops. She wrote enthusiastically about various productions she'd attended like Othello with Mademoiselle Grisi as Desdemona or what she called a 'mouth-watering production' of Les Sylphides.

The Vicar read one of her letters aloud to me, 'What an interesting and well-rounded young lady she is becoming. Just think, she's been learning archery of all things. We must hope such activities don't cause our girl to become too muscular.'

It was Mr. Coltman's oft-repeated wish for me to travel down to the south of England to present myself in person as a mother to my daughter. However, it took some pondering over the expediency of such an expedition before I felt ready to leave Lucy Brownrigg to take charge of the Keldgate shop with the help of her two eldest children.

A particularly suitable opportunity arose on receipt of a letter from Harriet informing me she was to travel with the Brooke family to stay at Lady Georgiana's London residence for a week. As soon as I was cognizant of Mr. and Mrs. Brooke's intimacy with the Duke and Duchess of Carlisle, I consulted Debrett's 'Peerage of England' found in Rev. Coltman's library; it listed countless Devonshires and Carlisles. Lady Georgiana was the wife of George Howard, the 6th Earl of Carlisle whose ancestral home was Castle Howard up here in Yorkshire. Her brother was the Duke of Devonshire and his country seat was Chatsworth House in Derbyshire where of course

Harriet had recuperated from the measles. He also owned the Londesborough Park estate which is not so far from here.

As inevitably I would be mixing with the 'beau monde' I took quite a bit of money from my account. I ignored the quizzical looks on the bank manager's wizened face as he ordered the clerk to count out fifty sovereigns from his copper shovel. Unlike some banks whose notes could only be used in the locality, Machell's had an arrangement with a London Bank to honour their £5 notes so I made sure I also had plenty of them to roll tightly inside my reticule. Selecting which gowns to take with me for such a momentous journey took a great deal of time as did the packing of my trunk. I decided on understated elegance and expensive jewellery à la Mrs. Siddons.

For the first part of the journey my mind was a ferment of agitation over the wisdom of my decision to venture anywhere at all. Due to Lucy living in the house adjoining mine, I would hear crashing and shouting at all hours. Her eldest son's great activity of body caused me to voice a few worries about damage to my property but she promised faithfully to confine her wild offspring to the backroom and never let them be alone in the shop.

As we drew nearer to London my greater worry was how would my relationship with Harriet fare? How should I greet her? Would an embrace be awkward? I'd informed her that I would take a room at Coopers Hotel in Bouverie Street relying on Rev. Coltman's assurance it was a suitable lodging for a respectable single lady. A Hackney carriage deposited me at the entrance and my luggage taken care of by an ostler; the carriage driver had refused to get it down in retaliation for my proffering the correct fare exactly, with no tip.

The following morning a note was brought to me suggesting a rendezvous in Park Square near Regents Park. I wore my dark red sarsenet which had emerged from the trunk not too badly creased. Checking my reticule held plenty of coins as well as my vinaigrette and fan I took a chair to ensure arriving unflustered. The springs of some of those chaises leave a lot to be desired and I had not recovered from the rudeness of the Hackney driver. After introductions and polite observations about the journey and the weather we made our plans for the day. Mrs Brooke was keen for the girls to see the 'Diorama' which had been erected in the Park just the year before. She was a woman in possession of plenty of opinions.

Thankfully our first encounter had passed easily with Harriet displaying a sweetness of temper I'd never observed previously. Mrs. Brooke declared she was convinced all the houses in London must be quite empty as everyone was out in the Parks. She looked directly at me as if expecting praise for such a sagacious observation. She was disobliged.

Harriet placed her hand in mine as we strolled to the entrance of the show. It cost a 1/- to get in but well worth all that money. Spectators were contained in a dark, circular room rather like a theatre without actors yet furnished with boxes and a pit. The whole saloon moved by some mechanical contrivance which brought curiously-lit, colourful pictures into view before disappearing once more. One was a depiction of a volcanic eruption on Mount Etna, another a handsome German Castle both 70 feet wide and 50 feet high. I'd never seen anything like it in the whole of my life. Despite being older, the Brooke girls were rather nervous but Harriet was completely unfazed.

In view of us having just witnessed a volcanic eruption, when we emerged, I felt compelled to regale the party with the tale of Mr. Fox confusing Rev. Coltman when speaking of the smoke coming through the fissures and the Vicar believing he was speaking of smoked fish. Mr. Brooke laughed heartily; Mrs. Brooke did not see the joke. She haughtily proposed we should seek something that would be more congenial to the girls.

I suggested perhaps the Zoological Gardens would suit as I had a fancy to see the monkeys, but they'd been there previously and had acquired the 30-page catalogue as a souvenir. After sitting in the dark for so long, Harriet looked for more lively entertainment although what she proposed was a visit to a pavilion housing a dead whale, wittily known as the 'Palace of the Prince of Whales'. For this we had to venture down steep steps to tables and chairs actually set right inside the creature's vast skeleton, 'confessed and exposed' and 'perfect in all its ossal anatomy' as it said in the description. It was estimated to be 85 feet long. Hence when I saw the 60-foot Sperm Whale displayed at Burton Constable Hall near Beverley a few years later I was less impressed, albeit there they had articulated the creature's ribs to spread out like some enormous fan. It had so amused me to see visiting children swinging from its lower jaw.

Lady Georgiana had graciously permitted Mrs. Brooke to ask me to take afternoon tea with her at their town house. As the girls ran off to the nursery, we ladies sat in the drawing room, enjoying genteel conversation. Thanking Providence for the inestimable value of once being patronised by Mrs. Sarah Siddons, I replicated my memory of her voice and posture to suit the occasion. Her recommendation was that one should not to seek to portray truth but rather a way of feeling. Therefore, that day I decided to feel like an aristocrat.

You can imagine my gratification when Lady Georgiana told me how very fond her family had become of my daughter, particularly her own dear Elizabeth who was about the same age. Lady Georgiana had 12 children, and also a sister named Harriet who they called 'Harryo'. The coincidence of names seemed to bring pleasure to a family famously accustomed to living ill together.

 I'm endeavouring to find a polite way of describing their irregularities but I fear I cannot. It is common knowledge that Lady Georgiana's mother lived with her husband and his mistress in a ménage à trois, while carrying on an affair with Prime Minister Charles Grey with whom she had a daughter, brought up by his parents. Knowing Lady G. senior had not seen her children for two years when she left England, helped me feel vindicated in my own decision to send Harriet away.

Members of the nobility and the government have become accustomed to constant ridicule in the press for their immorality and spendthrift ways. And modern playwrights such as my Mr. Richard Sheridan cleverly reflected popular opinion by continually poking fun at society families. For instance, it is widely accepted that it was the older Lady Georgiana he had lampooned when creating the character of Lady Sneerwell in his 'School for Scandal'.

Being a guest in one of the smaller houses owned by such a noble family served to demonstrate the vast gulf between my childhood experiences and that of my daughter who appeared so easily settled into such a refined circle. I got the impression that Harriet's distress at the rows and giddiness usual in the Howard household, led to a general improvement in behaviour amongst the siblings. Even the youngest, Mary, whose wilfulness exasperated everyone, could be charmed out of bed by Harriet when she refused to bestir herself for her maid or her mother. Lady Georgiana actually remarked that Harriet's presence brought an unusual amiability to her children none of whom owned a submissive temper. It crossed my mind that knowing nothing but unbounded prosperity doubtlessly influenced their dispositions.

Despite her outrageous family, her Ladyship possessed a most cordial manner. She quizzed me closely about Beverley as her husband had just become Lord Lieutenant of the East Riding. When she let slip that he had been a close friend of George Canning, I felt emboldened to describe being a passive spectator of the duel between him and Lord Castlereagh. Lady Georgiana's hand flew to her mouth covering her gasp before demanding to know more. Obediently I gave full rein to my description of the place, the morning, the wound and the senseless behaviour of men. I was surprised how enthusiastically she agreed with me about this last observation. Mrs. Brooke said very little.

We also shared opinions on books we'd read. She surprised me by dismissing every one of Mr. Charles Dickens works, calling him a 'sentimental socialist' and declared she had no wish to encounter pickpockets and disreputable women when reading for pleasure. We parted on the best of terms.

Back in Beverley, although there was little about which to complain in the way Lucy had looked after the shop in my absence, I decided it was in my best interest to employ someone to manage it on a regular basis, having now acquired a taste for socialising. I found a suitable candidate in Mr. Samuel Carter who lived in Lairgate and, by entrusting him with a key to the shop door, my customary early rising for start of business became a thing of the past. There is such pleasure in being able to turn over and relish another hour or so in bed.

The following year Harriet was invited to travel north with Lady Georgiana and her family to stay at their country house in Yorkshire, Castle Howard. I wrote to her Ladyship saying how much I'd enjoyed our 'conversazione' in London and requesting an opportunity to see my daughter whilst she was in the vicinity. Almost by return post I received a note written by a housekeeper saying that I may make arrangements to visit the following week and suggesting a coaching inn for an overnight stay.

In a hired chaise with my brother Bill, his wife Amy with their nine-year old Amelia, we travelled along the narrow meandering lanes of North Yorkshire, swaying alarmingly around sharp curves. It was particularly hazardous whenever other vehicles travelled toward us and there was no option for Bill but to rein back sharply. Little Amelia clung to her Mother like a limpet which in turn upset Amy as she became increasingly dishevelled.

We took rooms at the Worsley Arms and set off the next day to pay our visit to the great house. Not as early as I would have wished as Amy liked the morning well-aired before she got up. I wore my pale lilac silk while Amy selected her good deal worn, unsuitable pink, desperately at odds with her florid cheeks. She knew nothing of taste. But little Amelia looked bonny in a hand-me-down from my Harriet.

In order to penetrate the great estate of Castle Howard we took a straight but undulating carriageway passing through tidily cultivated areas interspersed with others left wild and darkly mysterious. How blessed this family was in possession of such a house whose absolute perfection had taken over a hundred years to achieve.

Blanche and Elizabeth Carlisle insisted on showing us around scores of beautifully furnished rooms without any of the rigid formality you may have expected. Harriet took little Amelia out into the gardens to get to know her cousin and to play with some spaniel puppies. I imagined the Carlisle children acquired their self-assurance at their school in London, where, they informed us an actual coach was installed in a back room so girls could be trained to get in and out elegantly.

Several generations of the Howard family gazed down on us as we ascended the Great Staircase. Famous artists had recorded centuries of extravagant fashions - beards and ruffs, gargantuan wigs and stiff gowns. Along corridors we marched, passing the sculpted stone heads of deceased male Carlisles disposed on plinths. Shutters open in the upstairs Drawing Room allowed the sun to beam on the white and gilt paintwork and feature the cumulation of cobwebs hanging from stags' heads, shot long ago.

The explanation for the continuing success of these noble families suddenly became clear to me: it's their familiarity with their ancestry. Everything about their history has been recorded for them on paper and preserved in paintings and sculptures. They can build on what their families already possess with scant jeopardy. As for me, a single woman, I have nothing but my own very particular talents.

Bill observed Castle Howard should be named Howard Palace and speculated on cellars full of Burgundy and stables full of hunters. The pillars, the furniture, the paintings and elegant ceilings all deserved more attention than we had time to give. I could only marvel at the way Harriet appeared completely at home in such awe-inspiring surroundings while my brother and his wife gawped silently and unashamedly, nudging one another and pointing.

As we took tea with her housekeeper in a minor drawing room dominated by a painting the size of my parlour wall, Lady Georgiana looked in on us sporting a feather-trimmed satin jockey cap. After an affable greeting, she apologised for having no time for conversation as quite unexpectedly, she had a pressing engagement which could not be put off. Effortlessly drawing on my acting ability, I exchanged a few civilities as became a lady intimate with the upper classes, sensing Bill and Amy exchanging glances behind my back. The following day we set off back to Beverley taking Harriet with us.

Chapter 14

Farewell to Miss Harriet Fox

I had hoped that this would be an appropriate time for me to reacquaint Harriet with the place of her birth. Unhappily the stark contrast between the rampant riches of Castle Howard and the back streets of Beverley proved too much for her to accept. The racket of passing carts and carriages or indeed nauseous smells permeating the area from the tanneries was not what she was accustomed to. Her room in my house adjoining the shop was smaller and plainer than any she had known in recent years and she was dismayed to discover I did not even possess a goat-cart. Several times she remarked how much colder it was here than in the south of England; the weather during her stay certainly was unseasonal. But I suspected the main source of her discomfiture was the mere fact of us being alone together for any length of time.

For all Lady Georgiana's praise of my daughter's facility for bringing peace and happiness, I found no evidence for such a thing. There was still so little we agreed upon. I liked to take walks across the Westwood, breathing in God's good clean air; she preferred shopping. Although we both loved reading and the theatre, our tastes were at variance.

I showed her around the Minster which she said was similar to Westminster Abbey but not so grand. I wondered if she would care to demonstrate her skill at archery when I took her up to the Butts. She confessed that in her letters she had exaggerated her prowess, having never once succeeding in getting an arrow to even stick in the target. She had no wish to be considered a toxophilite she said disdainfully.

On seeing a notice announcing a visit to the town of a famous Tenting Circus, I thought I'd found the very thing to entertain my daughter. For one week the whole town had eagerly awaited the erection of the great tent but boisterous weather had prevented it. Heavy rain caused the elephants' wagon to become so embedded in thick mud in Pighill Lane that eventually it had to be dragged out by teams of borrowed horses watched by cheering crowds enjoying the free entertainment. When all was ready, we stood at the roadside watching a cacophanous brass band lead a procession of elephants, camels, horses and clowns through the town to the 'Splendid Novel Pavilion' where the spectacular show was to take place.

'I don't think I care for clowns very much Mama,' said Harriet, shuddering as some came too close for her liking.

'Ah, but when you see them in action in the circus ring with their famous 'performing Hippo' you will have a very different opinion I have no doubt,' I reassured. How deflating then to find that this placarded 'wonder' turned out to be merely an inflated skin on a long stick waved about by each clown in turn. The one thing I was certain would bring a smile to Harriet's face turned out to be a complete sell.

The performance we attended was the third one that day. My opinion as a professional actress was that constant repetition of their routines by the rouged tumblers and tinselled dancers had resulted in weariness and downright apathy in the troupe. People in my theatre company had often complimented me on the freshness of my performance no matter how often I delivered the same lines. But here bored Chinese jugglers were followed by demonstrations of trick-riding on horseback executed by Friday-faced women shamelessly exhibiting their legs. This did elicit excited whistles from men in the audience watching from behind the barrier; we were left quite unmoved. When the shiny top hat was passed round, Harriet rebuked me for putting in a whole sovereign but I felt a twinge of sorrow for those forced into such demeaning employment perhaps through being discharged penniless from the armed forces

Straight after breaking our fast the following morning, having cast about for anything to interest my daughter, I said, 'I know the very thing we must do today. We will have an expedition to view the inheritance your father left you.'

Visibly taken aback Harriet groaned, 'Do we have to Mama? Is it far? I don't really know if I want to own property around here.'

'It's yours whether you wish it or not and It will be amusing to take the ferry across the River Hull and explore your land in the mystic village of Weel. It weel be an adventure,' I joked, endeavouring to inject some enthusiasm into my proposition. I did realise her streak of waywardness was the most obvious trait she had inherited from me.

With poor grace, Harriet wrapped herself up in her warmest clothes, not believing the weather could ever be anything but chill and dull here. The boy was dispatched to get us a gig and off we trundled to the Grovehill ferry. Despite her foreboding and squeals of fear we got to the landing place at the other side of the River Hull in but a few minutes, completely unscathed. Harriet clung tightly to my arm, professing a queasiness brought on by the barely rippling water. Without doubt this was another flaw in her nature passed on from me, but this stream was but a puddle compared to the Thames and the Humber.

We made our way from the landing stage to view her properties but were soon forced to walk apart, arms splayed wide for balance to safely negotiate the rutted lanes. Mr. Fox had been so proud when he became the owner of a country estate. He boasted of the way he had out-flanked the former owner, Mr. Pelham whose arrogance and high-handedness was to be expected from anyone connected by marriage to the prestigious Wharton family. Regrettably the acres of water meadows and dykes failed to impress Harriet. Only a farmhouse named 'Butterbump Hall' caused her any amusement; we did not delay our journey home.

Back in the chaise I asked her, 'Now you have become a country landowner you must decide how to proceed. Do you plan to appoint a land agent?'

'I cannot say Mama, I have no notion of such things,' was the reply.

'How will you collect the rents and which bank will you choose?' I persisted.

'How can I tell? I fear I never will be suited to such a position. I truly believe that you should have the management and responsibility. Yes, that is the answer. I will hand over my bequest to you and you can restore it to me when I become more responsible.'

'If you are sure that is what you wish then so be it,' I shrugged in a blatantly reluctant manner. You can see that I put absolutely no pressure upon my daughter to hand over the property, whatever some may say. No one could doubt that Harriet was destined to make a good marriage, being beautiful, educated and personable. What need would she ever have of a private income?

'No, I am absolutely certain that this is for the best. I know Mr. Fox was very generous in leaving me such a large estate but my only wish now is to return to the south of England. I'm certain I can never feel comfortable here,' said Harriet.

The day before Mr. and Mrs. William Coltman had undertaken to take Harriet back down to Bromley, we spent in sorting out her belongings. Harriet chattered interminably as we went through toys and books that Mr. Fox had carefully preserved from her early childhood. Having looked over the relics of her past, she exhibited no attachment to them whatsoever and bade me give everything to the poor children of the town. There was a trunk full of her beautiful little dresses which I suppose could still be surviving somewhere, perhaps cut up for clippy rugs.

'Now Mama I insist you have something to remember me by. Here are my precious stones and shells as I thought you would wish to have them. And I'm going to leave you that little box of coins and this drawing. Now do take care of the shells and stones as they are very tender things. And I've done another little drawing for Mr. Coltman as it will make a pair to the one I sent him before. It's only a scribble I did in a few minutes'.

I've had her drawings neatly framed, one for me and one for Rev. Coltman. Those wretched shells still languish in a cupboard somewhere here in Albany House; I can't really throw them out though, can I?

Patently relieved by release from her enforced Beverley exile, Harriet waved enthusiastically to me from the Coltman's carriage early the next morning. That was the last I ever saw of her although we continued to communicate fairly regularly. Having observed my life in Beverley, I believe Harriet had concluded I must be dreadfully poor for she kindly proposed a scheme for saving me money by sending me messages for which I wouldn't have to pay. She told me that if she addressed a letter to 'Mrs Elizabeth Taylor' I should pay for it at the Post Office in Toll Gavel; it would mean there was something particular she wanted to communicate. If it was merely directed to 'Mrs. E. Taylor' I should understand that she was thinking of me and keeping well but needed nothing so there was no need to part with money to read it, although I usually did.

Unbeknown to my daughter I was taking steps to ensure I would continue to be comfortably off in my dotage. In the weeks after she left, I took it upon myself to visit all the farmsteads and particularly the Ferry Inn in Weel village to ascertain and adjust the rents upwards and sat back in expectation of an assured steady income from Harriet's legacy. I also ventured into buying stocks in Harriet's name; there was no risk as, being under the age of twenty-one, she would have had no liability for any debts. And the dividends paid for her care with the Brooke family.

Harriet had another ploy to save me from expending money for four sheets of notepaper was, when she had lots of news, she wrote it all on a single page. Once she had covered one side, she would give the page a quarter turn and write across what she'd already written then do the same on the back. This drove me quite wild as I found it so difficult to read. Oftentimes I had to take it up to Rev. Coltman at the Vicarage for him to disentangle. Being used to deciphering ancient documents, he had a peculiar facility for sorting out the words, but at times even he needed to employ his quizzing glass in order to tell me what Harriet had been about.

It was one such letter which informed me that Harriet and her companions were suffering the dreaded whooping cough. Reverend Coltman read out, 'Please do not worry my dear Mother as this mild weather is driving the hooping cough away and we have all been much better lately we were to have gone to Sandisted but feared giving it to Mr. Courtneys little girl who had not had it'

'Oh, the dear child how thoughtful she is,' Mr. Coltman beamed across to me.

I was concerned but as the next part of the letter was all about going to concerts and to London to get new frocks and petticoats, I decided things could not be too bad and happily joined the Vicar in the consumption of tea and cakes. Just to be on the safe side I did send a note to Mrs. Brooke asking her to get an apothecary to apply some leeches to Harriet's neck and to try dosing her with Daffy's elixir.

This was the last letter I got from her - 'My dear Mother I have this morning received your letter and the brooch which I am very much obliged to you for and though I have got a little turquoise brooch I think it will be very nice for a change My tooth powder box has at last opened and I have used some of the contents which I dare say are very good but I have not been able to try it long Believe me your affectionate daughter Harriet Fox.'

My disgruntlement with her lack of gratitude for the brooch I'd taken such care in selecting quickly waned when I saw that one of the Miss Shepherds had written on the space next to the address, the horrid information that 'Harriet wouldn't tell you but she was coughing a lot and wasn't well but said she had no pain.' As you may imagine it was quite a shock when the next letter I received was to ask about arrangements for my daughter's funeral. She was only sixteen years of age.

It turned out that all Harriet's property came to me when she passed away as her next of kin but quite unaccountably, due to some legal nicety, the copyhold of Weel reverted to the Lord of the Manor. I was furious and instructed my solicitor to take action on my behalf and eventually I did get it restored to my name. If this was what helped Mr. Welburn to decide I would be a suitable wife, I could not say, but if that was so, it back-fired; I outlived him and became the very wealthy widow you see now.

Chapter 15

Death, Destruction and Deviance

I felt overwhelmingly obliged to attend to Harriet's funeral arrangements in person despite the daunting prospect of a miserable journey alone down to London. It being beyond Reverend Coltman's abilities to repeatedly get in and out of a coach, I was tempted to ask Gillyatt Sumner to accompany me, knowing he was always eager to visit that city of high fashion. But would he have provided me with any emotional support on the journey? In any event I was disinclined to make an approach having not spoken to him for almost a year owing to his involvement in a series of disgraceful scenes in the Minster,

You may remember me telling you about the Churchwarden's long-simmering dispute coming to its zenith when Mr. Plaxton took the decision to reduce the Churchwardens' Pew to only five stalls. Hence at every single service in the Minster, the Churchwardens of St. Johns and St. Martins felt it behoved them to quarrel over their right to sit in it so as not to lose face. Drink had usually been consumed at the Hall Garth Inn previously.

Gilly called the Churchwardens of St. Martins 'a bunch of drinking, dancing fools' which prompted Mr. Plaxton to hold a clenched fist to his face and threaten to throw him over the Pew and kick him out. Those queuing for St. John's Bread one Sunday heard someone bawl at Gilly, 'Thou nasty dirty rascal I have a good mind to punch thy arse. I never buggered George Smith's lad as thou did.' Others reported a St. Martins man had pulled a St. Johns man out of his seat shouting, 'You scoundrel you have got my seat and you got my seat last Sunday. If you come here again, I will kick you all out of the Pew and give you unto custody of our constable.' And all this in the sacred precincts of the Minster!

Gillyatt complained bitterly about the insults he had suffered but rather than merely demanding an apology, aggravated the matter further by insisting the Ecclesiastical Court should deal with it. He was particularly annoyed when Reverend Coltman stubbornly refused to take any action himself against the St. Martins Churchwardens, cravenly saying 'There is lack of witnesses to prove any point of this case.' Which I'm afraid, was not strictly accurate.

Inexorably addicted to litigation and the excitement of the Courtroom, over the years Gilly had employed every single solicitor in Beverley to obtain compensation or apologies for the myriad insults and assaults he regularly received. The disagreement about the ownership of the Pew he regarded as a personal affront and immediately commissioned Mr. Empson to tell the Magistrates, 'It may be remarked that Mr. Plaxton had the Churchwarden's Pew made smaller for the purpose of annoyance and that he had been in several scrapes on account of his quarrelsome temper. Mr. Sumner indignantly denies the charges of unnatural offences and claims his moral character has never been impeached.'

The Magistrates' decision to bind over Mr. Plaxton and Mr. Nutchey for £50 to keep the peace Gilly took to mean that he, personally, was absolved of any blame.

After deliberation I concluded a long coach journey with him could only prove detrimental to my mood, knowing his delight in stirring up contention wherever he went. Furthermore, Mr. and Mrs. Brooke certainly did not possess the faculty to appreciate his acid type of badinage. Therefore, to London I travelled, alone.

The Brookes were very understanding about my wish for Harriet to be buried with her father at Beverley Minster. Together we arranged a simple commemorative service in a small church in London to enable her friends and acquaintances to pay their respects. With Mr. and Mrs. William Coltman they chose the coffin and the hymns and advised me on the hire of a funeral cart to transport Harriet's body back to Beverley.

Hoping to distract myself from further melancholy, I stayed on in London for a few days to re-visit my old haunts. On the evening before my return to East Yorkshire, I'd walked further than I'd intended. Being October, darkness soon came and as the fog drifted in off the Thames the lamps struggled to illuminate the foot pavements to any great effect. Not a single link-boy was to be found to carry a torch for me.

Though well-acquainted with London from my walks with Michael Macready, somehow the street vendors' calls and rattling carriages distracted me from noticing where my feet were taking me. I struggled to divert my thoughts from the unaccustomed desolation of losing a child as hot tears spontaneously blurred my eyes. Empty and bereft with head bowed and teeth chattering, I suddenly found myself looking round, desperately trying to recall the way back to my Inn. And there I was, inadvertently standing right next to the Houses of Parliament. It must have been over twenty years since I'd entered that very building with Mr. John Bellingham.

As I stood looking up at that historic pile, a stooped woman shuffled past, the first person I'd seen for some time. Clutching an unwieldy basket piled with faggots, she seemed unaware of them falling out behind her as she made her way into the building by way of a small dark door. I followed her, gathering up what she'd dropped. She carried on down gloomy stairs leading to a basement where two workmen stood by brightly blazing furnaces.

One said 'Hello there, Mrs. Wright! Now who's this fine young lady you've brought down here to see us?' The woman whipped round, seeming astonished at finding me just behind her.

'Sorry, if I startled you, but you were dropping all this kindling, I thought you may need it,' and I showed her what I'd picked up.

'Well you'd better throw 'em in there then.' She indicated the furnace giving out least warmth. One of the men said, 'Don't stand there looking as cold as last night's porridge, come a bit closer my lady.'

'You can't be a Cockney, speaking like that,' I smiled, feeling a lot warmer and happier at having something else to think about and actual human beings with whom to converse; I find that's always the best way to expunge death or disappointment. The man appeared kindly despite wearing a face puckered from the pox.

'No madam, we're two fine Irish lads, come across the sea to the big city to make names for ourselves, you know. Plenty of jobs here in London and this one is well-paid and warm, isn't it now, Benjamin?' The other fellow nodded and kept throwing more sticks into the fire causing it to die back a bit.

'Surely no one pays you just to keep a fire going. I could do a job like that.' To me the notion was ridiculous.

'Important work this is. It's for the Government, I'll have you know. There's two cart loads of tally sticks here and we've been ordered to burn them all. We need lots of faggots to help them catch hold. Surplus to requirements they are now the Treasury has decided to stop using them to tally up their accounts. It's all written down in ledgers now in the modern way. Help us if you want, we'll pay you with a glass of ale, a meat pie and a bit of warmth,' said the first man.

'I'm grateful to you for your benevolence, Sir but it looks to me like your fire's going out,' said I. Benjamin swore roundly then went to get something to encourage the flames back, waddling off on bowed legs. Mam would've said 'he couldn't stop a pig in a passage with them legs.' He was soon back clutching a bottle which he uncorked and splashed the contents immoderately on to the embers as I threw the rest of my faggots into the darkening stove. In a matter seconds, flames burst forth with alarming fierceness, causing him to step back rapidly, leaving the furnace door open. I could see sparks flying across the room towards the thick curtains and in an instant they were afire. It was my dressing room at Drury Lane Theatre all over again! While the old lady was trying to beat out the flames with her basket, more started licking round the panelling. Hastily hitching up my skirts I ran back up the stairs as if the clappers of hell were after me.

From across the road, as I leant gasping against the railings, I saw the two Irish men watch Mrs. Wright lock the door securely behind her, so I knew they were safe. How I then got back to my lodgings I will never know; my wits being completely scattered by all the catastrophic events as well as the complexity of negotiating unfamiliar streets in semi-darkness. Once in my room my legs collapsed me on to the meagre bed in total exhaustion.

Thousands of Londoners had watched hundreds of volunteers bringing up every parish fire engine in the city and manned the pumps. The conflagration was in severe danger of totally consuming our seat of government. The fire that began with the burning of tally sticks spread along the winding passages and rambling staircases to the panelling in the Commons and as the curtains round Black Rod's box flared up, the Lords' Chamber was destroyed as well. As the majority of the population viewed the disaster to be a sign of God's displeasure at the passing of the Poor Law Amendment Act, happily no blame came to lie with those who may have been careless with the immolation of tally sticks!

And of course, that same year the House of Commons had plenty of other things to trouble their heads about. When King William dismissed his Prime Minister, Lord Melbourne after the fire, the Duke of Wellington was given the stop-gap appointment until the next election. He was still very popular for giving all ranks the 'Waterloo Medal' and pretending it had been a Great British Victory whereas in truth most of army were Prussian or Dutch. Then Parliament decreed that rather than the king choosing our Prime Ministers, a better policy would be for the Members of Parliament to make such an important decision. They chose Mr. Robert Peel who found himself without a majority and within six months Lord Melbourne was back once more in his old job. Such a brisk turnover of Prime Ministers meant they all managed to do nothing and so avoid anything which could accrue subsequent blame. The only good thing about 1834 was that Slavery was abolished.

Once back at home I judged it discreet to keep silent about having been present at the burning down of the House of Commons as well as of Drury Lane Theatre so as not to feed the furnace of blame that tended to follow me. I was preserved from dwelling on the disaster for too long being beset by the necessity of making the arrangements for Harriet's funeral at the Minster.

Not many Beverley people knew Harriet but they certainly knew me. Would they think she was my god-daughter or my bastard child? Would I be pitied or scorned? The service was quite well attended. Reverend Coltman officiated but could barely speak for weeping into his large handkerchief. She was buried in her pink pedmarine frock in her father's grave as he would have wished.

Chapter 16

A History of Reverend Joseph Coltman,
The Heaviest Man in England

It is disappointing to relate that for all Reverend Coltman's outstanding erudition, it seemed it counted for nothing compared to his fame for being the heaviest man in England since Daniel Lambert.

This grieved him; his passion was to educate and inspire others to learn but, sadly, many couldn't see past his vast bulk. He knew more about the History of Beverley Minster than anyone in the whole world. Over the years Mr. Coltman had ferreted out and deciphered old documents and records stored away in the repositories of the Minster and the Guild Hall. He loved nothing better than telling stories from the past, as you will appreciate if you go to view his commemorative tablet on the wall in the north aisle of the Minster. It praises 'his peculiar felicity in communicating knowledge.'

I came to expect any conversation with him would include a reference to the contribution he and Mr. Fox had made to Mr. Poulson's massive great tome entitled 'Beverlac or the Antiquities and History of the Town of Beverley'. Two of these hefty books remain wedged in my bookcase in Albany House as both Mr. Fox and Mr. Welburn were subscribers; I must get round to reading one.

It was Rev. Coltman who transcribed much of the information about St. John's miracles, responsible for attracting thousands of pilgrims to Beverley over the centuries. You cannot believe the gullibility of people in the past. There is one story about King William the Conqueror's soldiers trying to steal gold bracelets from an old man in the Churchyard; straightaway St. John caused him to fall stone dead from his horse, his head completely twisted round the wrong way. And there was a boy killed after falling from the roof of the Minster who amazed the assembled crowd by immediately standing up, safe and uninjured. Also, a man who had never walked in his life, fell asleep propped up against St. John's tomb; on waking he found he could march about the Church, impelled to sing praises to the Lord God.

Sceptics will tell you that such stories always appeared whenever the Provost and the Canons of the Minster lacked the money for repairs to the Church and decided glad tidings of miracles would encourage more pilgrims to visit the town, offering benevolences. It certainly worked a treat for the splendid building still stands proudly here today does it not? And who would ever blame those ancient churchmen for exploiting St. John's reputation if it was to the benefit of the Church?

All the time I knew him, Reverend Coltman found great difficulty in walking because of his weight. He preferred his hobby horse to his carriage for circumnavigating his parish, it being a more convenient way to speak to his flock. One of his servants or I would walk beside him after he once fell into a ditch and became extremely distressed at being unable to clamber out.

The Vicar would make a point of stopping in the Market Place to speak to the 'Babes in the Wood', his name for the lads locked into the stocks. He would ask how they'd come to be in such trouble then give them his blessing whereupon they would look up at him in remorseful fashion and tell him a load of bouncers. If you looked back, they'd be sniggering at the sight of such a fat man. I heard one clever sod say 'If a pound of mutton candles cost seven pence-halfpenny, how much do you reckon that God-botherer would cost?'

No one can speak of the Reverend Coltman without recalling that famous hobby horse of his. He'd engaged Osgerby's coach builders to make one for him to get around the town after he'd grown so immense that sedan-chair men bluntly refused to even try to carry him. The congregation became used to the sight of the Vicar trundling the hobby horse along the Minster nave. The Churchwardens arranged a stout board sloping up into the pulpit and three Vergers would rush him up so he could stand there to preach his sermon, stuck in as tight as a candle in a candlestick. Eventually when that too became impossible, a desk was set beside the pulpit for him to carry on telling the congregation how to behave.

It was two years after Harriet's death that Rev. Coltman died. I still miss him. Because he made his will only the day before his demise, I believe he had a premonition of his imminent mortality, after all he had the same initials as Jesus Christ. His manservant, George Emley, got the blame for allowing Rev. Coltman to suffocate in his bed. He was employed to turn the Vicar over regularly in the night, being too large to do it for himself but George had fallen asleep on duty. He moved to Pocklington.

What a huge turnout there was for the funeral, though nothing like the 20,000 people we heard had turned up for Mr. Beethoven's in Vienna. I sat next to Gilly Sumner in his immaculate black velvet coat. His ambition to be a leader of fashion sadly met with little competition in Beverley. I'd brought forth my mourning dress once more from the depths of a weather-beaten calf-skin trunk once owned by Mr. Fox. I asked Polly to hang it outside in the breeze for an hour or so to dispel the smell of camphor. Her mam had to let out two seams as I wished to be able to breathe.

Gillyatt and I had assumed more friendly terms after Harriet's funeral but I was moved to express my surprise at his presence at this one for, as you know, he'd never had a single good word to say about Rev. Coltman. Gilly explained he was attending purely as a matter of respect but he continued to bring up his usual complaints about the Vicar always concurring with the St. Martins Churchwardens just because he'd nominated them. His refusal to allow Gillyatt to inspect the Parish Records had convinced him there must be something dreadful and improper to be found in them.

All shops closed on the day of Rev. Coltman's funeral. Our Bill's stone truck was necessary to move the extra-large coffin from the Vicarage to the churchyard for lowering into the ground with block and tackle and some wood poles. Gillyatt invited himself up to my house for a dish of tea after the obsequies. He let me know of his disgruntlement with my brother's generosity in not charging for the stone truck for the internment. It turned out our Bill had charged Gilly an extortionate price for hiring it when he wanted to transport the redundant medieval Guild Hall doorway to his house in Woodmansey. Bill would never do Gillyatt Sumner any favours.

To divert Gilly from this matter and his usual cruel aspersions on Rev. Coltman, I enquired about the black eye and swollen lip he'd been sporting in Church. Inevitably he was cock-a-hoop about his 'malicious beating' from Ben Reynolds for, after first threatening him with prosecution, he had accepted an abject and public apology. The antipathy, assaults and attacks he received would distress anyone else but Gillyatt. He derived an absurd sense of triumph from eliciting damages or listening to statements of contrition. Sensing my lack of support for his conduct, Gillyatt soon finished his tea, wetly kissed my hand and left, no doubt to antagonize someone else.

Now he has plenty of time in Bradford Gaol to reflect and regret. And you may have supposed with him out of the way, dissension within the Minster would have ceased. Sadly, this has not proved to be the case for two subsequent Vicars have suffered even worse vilification not only from their Churchwardens but also from people in the town. Reverend Ram actually had mud thrown at him in his expensive barouche when he banned the Bread Distribution to the poor on Perambulation Day. And now we have a Vicar being criticised for wanting to close down taverns proximate to the Minster in the belief the demon drink was solely to blame for his Churchwardens' unchristian behaviour.

Chapter 17

Coronation and Calamity

The year after Rev. Coltman's death, King William IV followed him, whether to heaven or not, who knows. At 64 William had been the oldest person ever to have been crowned king. Relying on the Duke of Wellington's advice he'd kept down the cost of his festivities to a mere £30,000; quite niggardly when compared to his brother George's £240,000 coronation costs. It would have been such a waste to have spent more as he only reigned for seven years.

We didn't do much celebrating here; Sunday School children sang a few hymns in Wednesday Market, processed to the Methodist chapel for a scrimped sermon before enjoying a bun in the Corn Exchange. Men took the opportunity to consume as much ale as possible to wish 'Good health to King William and Queen Adelaide!' No one mentioned his dozen or so bastards but several tankards may have been raised to them as well.

So, after a succession of disappointing male Hapsburgs and with King William having no legitimate children, we anticipated a brighter future under Queen Victoria. Hurrah! This time a woman was destined to rule the waves so we could now hope for reasonable behaviour from a monarch. When the Queen ignored Prime Minister Robert Peel's request to dismiss her Ladies of the Bedchamber as they were mostly wives of Whig MPs, he felt compelled to resign. How wonderful to have such power over men.

We'd been due to have a Queen a few years ago, but tragically Princess Charlotte had died in childbirth the year after I lost my Harriet. I consider myself most fortunate to have had a friend like Lucy Brownrigg delivering my baby as her natural instincts were demonstrably more successful than the methods of those 'learned doctors' who had attended the Princess. Their dissension and disagreements over the use of forceps to extract the royal bairn persisted so long that the outcome was two days of agonising labour, a still born child and death of the heiress to the throne, the only child begotten by Queen Caroline and the Prince Regent. Needless to say, there were some who could not believe he had any part in the begetting.

The start of the new reign seemingly changed the mood of the country; it coincided with hundreds of new inventions appearing to improve our drab lives life. Machinery has intervened to take over the drudgeries of sewing and weaving; we have the electrical telegraph, steam boats and mechanical reapers. Thousands of folk could now travel into London on railway trains to celebrate the accession of the new queen. Crowds overwhelmed the Royal Parks to marvel at balloon ascents and dazzling firework displays, much to the annoyance of all those who normally slept peacefully there under the trees.

Once more Beverley appeared quite apathetic as this next big royal event approached. No official plans for celebrations were announced until just a month before the big day. But this time the regular commonalty had their own ideas and rallied to the occasion. On Coronation Day bells rang from all the churches and banners flew from their towers. I did my part, propping up some dusty flags in my shop window and closing for the day. By mid-morning the town was in a complete bustle as different parties began to move to the Guild Hall to make up a procession.

None of your high-ranking Tories joined it nor did a single clergyman of the established church nor even a single East Riding Magistrate. But they weren't missed. A band played, followed by scarlet coated militia, who'd been up on the Westwood every week practising marching with muskets or sturdy branches in lieu. How they would have scared Mr. Bonaparte! The Mayor and Council, civic officers, Liberal gentry plus respectable tradesmen and the Manchester Unity of Oddfellows followed behind.

Pennock Tigar's two sons led a hundred of his workmen struggling to hold up massive banners embroidered with gold crowns and mottoes such as 'England's Hope', 'Commerce & Agriculture', and 'Prosperity to Grovehill'! Mr. Tigar made a lot of money when he found chalk dug out from Queensgate quarry was perfect for making 'Paris White' whitewash.

Like all other major employers of the town, he aimed to provide the most generous celebrations for his workers. Commodious booths were erected for the consumption of roast beef, plum pudding and brown ale. Everyone took home a Coronation Bun; I dare say some still lie fossilised in cupboards, saved for posterity. George Hudson, popularly known as the 'Railway King', went even further with his munificence on the Queen's birthday. He organised a Grand Parade in York and provided a dinner for 14,000 people. Beyond any doubt there is money to be made from railways.

The Coronation brought throngs of people to Westwood Common for sports, music and dancing, parties and shows, leaving the town centre quite deserted. No doubt it was highly gratifying to every lover of order and tradition to see this enthusiastic display of loyal feeling for our new monarch. For my part, squibs and firecrackers bouncing and firing every evening for weeks, quite wearied me.

Just how much conviviality and joy can be merited for an accident of birth that made some woman a Queen? I know Rev. Thurlow had gone to the trouble of preparing a sermon on the 'Divine Origin of Regal Power' but whoever believes in such a thing nowadays? Wasn't Victoria a human being like the rest of us? Any woman surely would suffer sitting through the five-hour ceremony on a benumbing throne and having the Coronation Ring forced onto her stubby finger. Had she actually done anything to earn such a position and did she really want it?

I thought so hard about the Queen's position, I began to feel quite sorry for her. Perhaps I was the more fortunate woman as I now had choices, albeit not as many as a man. Emboldened by successfully and single-handedly managing a grocery and fruiterers, there was money and time to see more of the world.

As though fate had ordained it, when strolling through the Market Place my eye was drawn to an illustrated notice posted up near Greens shop announcing the sailing of the 'splendid and powerful steam vessel' the SS Forfarshire every Wednesday from Kingston-upon-Hull to the Scottish town of Dundee. It may strike you as rather odd that I nurtured a fancy to travel. Although I had crossed the Thames by wherry and the Humber by ferry with no great enjoyment, I decided this sea trip was the very thing I was looking for.

Beverley used to be a great port on the River Hull as you know but it was mainly fishing boats they built down at Grovehill, small enough to be launched sideways into the narrow river. The Humber caters for large vessels which of course is to the benefit of Hull where many are built.

The Forfarshire had been built in Dundee and had only been in service for 4 years. It was exceedingly smart. Not only did it have three boilers, but masts and sails were installed in case the boilers failed. I made a point of inquiring about the safety of such vessels, because soon after the paddle steamer 'Victoria' had been launched in Hull, her boiler blew up. The clerk disdainfully assured me there was absolutely no danger with the good ship Forfarshire; it was extraordinarily soundly built and in the hands of their most reliable captain.

My reasoning for booking a 'main cabin for £1.5s. with the assurance of luxurious accommodation' was this - should I decide the sea was not for me, the trip up to Dundee in Scotland wouldn't take so long and I could always come back home by coach. If on the other hand, I found I enjoyed the experience, I would have no hesitation of sailing further, perhaps to Belgium or Sweden. I knew it would be nothing like sailing to America but Scotland could almost be regarded as going abroad wouldn't you say?

It was pleasant sailing behind two other ships along the flat calm of the Humber estuary, seeing the trees and fields of Yorkshire and Lincolnshire drift by on either side and I experienced none of the dizzying sensations I'd felt on smaller boats. However, after the Humber pilots left us at Spurn Point the prospect dramatically altered. The raging North Sea began pushing and pulling the Forfarshire about, capriciously rising and falling, to the detriment of anyone attempting to traverse the deck. Even the sailors with their sea legs clung to the rails. The prospect of a serene sail along the coast evaporated.

With the sixty or so other passengers I withdrew below decks to settle in the comparative comfort of the saloon, happily escaping the torment of seasickness which even members of the crew were experiencing. Despite voices being raised above the noise from the engines and the clamour of the waves, I managed to hold a spasmodic conversation with two Russian gentlemen in broken English who, I believed, were encouraging me to travel with them to St. Petersburg. I excused myself and found a chair anchored beside a very affable Scottish lady, also travelling alone.

'And what brings you to brave the high seas by yourself?' she enquired. Her curious accent was but a shade easier to comprehend than that of the Russians.

'I must confess I had a sudden urge to escape the enforced jollity of Coronation Festivities,' I said. 'Well, if that's the case, Dundee is the place for you,' said she. 'There'll be very little unconfined joy there, I will assure you.'

To enable us to better comprehend the other's unaccustomed pronunciation, our heads drew closer together as we chatted and drank whisky. Her overuse of gillyflower water almost overwhelmed me but I am convinced she told me that she had 300 sovereigns sewn into the seams of her skirts. I may have misheard her for, although she spoke the Queen's English, some words she used were entirely foreign to me. Being unsure of attaining a good night's sleep we were in no hurry to retire to our respective cabins and I learned more than anyone would need to know of her home and family in Dundee. Surprisingly I found I slept well that first night, quite lulled by the movement and sounds of the ship and all the unaccustomed whisky.

My ears quickly adapted to the maritime sounds so it was quite a shock when on the second afternoon the engines suddenly went silent. It turned out the boilers had begun to leak soon after leaving Hull and the lashing rain had put out all the furnaces. As it was impossible to be served a meal at dining tables without it ending in one's lap, stewards brought food to each cabin. Officers also came round at regular intervals reassuring us that all was well and recommending we should stay where we were despite being thrown about in all directions. Each cabin was issued with a lidded pail in case the turbulence caused seasickness. The sails had been set so we could run out the storm and everything certainly would calm down soon or so they said.

However well-appointed my cabin was, after a few hours I felt I could not abide the thought of being trapped there alone any longer. Dressing myself in warm flannel underwear I put a wadded petticoat under my dark burgundy gown and then squeezed into my thick coat. Despite all these layers restricting my movement I stuffed everything of any value into my carpet bag, carefully securing its two locks before disobediently venturing up to the fore deck.

Spasmodic moonlight struggling through the worsening wind and rain indicated we were heading for a craggy shore. The consequent Inquiry established that by mistakenly identifying the Longstone Lighthouse as the Farne Lighthouse, Captain John Humble had directed the Forfarshire straight to disaster. But let us give the man the benefit of the doubt and trust he believed he was making the correct decision. Whoever would blame him for making an error in such difficult circumstances?

With a grinding shock the Forfarshire was pitched into the rocks and after an unearthly groaning and grating, quite incredibly the whole ship broke into two parts. From where I stood, clinging to the rail of the fore deck, I could see black boulders several feet below. On looking behind, I saw the aft of the ship being swept helplessly away. It took but a second for me to determine the best place for me was solid ground. As the deck rose then fell, I threw my bag as far as I could before climbing over the side and flung myself down, hoping my extra layers of clothing would billow out, in the manner of a hot air balloon and moderate my fall.

I was soon joined on the slippy rocks by the Ship's Carpenter who had come to the same conclusion as myself. We held on to each other tightly then saw a woman peering through the rails with two children clinging to her skirts. The Ship's Carpenter yelled at them to quickly jump down to us. The children were dangled then dropped, one at a time before the woman pitched herself forward and we hauled them all up away from the seething waves. In all thirteen people made it down on to land. Unfortunately the last four were not quick enough and almost immediately vanished into the maelstrom as we watched helplessly.

Our small group rapidly slid and scrambled up the rocks as far away from the sea as possible and clung together for warmth and protection.   My carpet bag was put to good use as a pillow. Unfortunately, there was no way of bringing warmth back to the children just by chafing their hands and holding them close. I don't believe their mother had the time to dress them suitably. Their little bodies shook violently with the chill until they suddenly stopped and we realised exposure to the cold and wet had caused them to quietly expire in our arms.

I had to slap the hysterical woman until she stopped screaming before hugging her to me all through that hellish night; I had never before held another woman in my arms.   After a few hours of shuddering sobs and inhalations of sal volatile Mrs. Dawson became calm as a Quaker. I had no way of knowing whether she slept or had slipped away herself. There was nothing to be done but sit there for hours in silent misery waiting for death to claim us too.

As dawn pushed back the night sky, the arrival of a small coble genuinely took us by surprise. A girl held on to the oars whilst the man with her shouted through his cupped hands, urging us to get down to the small boat without delay. I shook Mrs. Dawson until her eyes opened and she regained the horror of what had happened.

The surging sea constantly threatened to dislodge the boat from its rocky niche as the girl desperately tried to keep it steady.   Mrs. Dawson was loth to leave her children's bodies behind but the Ships Carpenter and I forced her to move, slipping and sliding on her backside towards our saviours. The boatman grabbed her arms and kept assuring her he would certainly come back for them once the living had been rescued. I followed clutching my carpet bag; my sodden skirts severely hampering my transfer into the comparative safety of the coble. Imagine if my Scottish friend been in the same position, the weight of hundreds of sovereigns sewn into her seams would have made it totally impossible for her to climb aboard a small boat.   Nine people escaped in a lifeboat dropped from the ship and nine of us were rowed from the rocks in two journeys made by the boatman and his daughter.

But you just go and ask anyone what they remember about that fateful day. Why it would be Miss Grace Darling of course! That young girl with long fair hair and beautiful blue eyes who rowed out in a small boat with her father into a terrible storm became our national heroine meriting poems, paintings and pottery all praising her bravery. A subscription was raised and Queen Victoria sent her £50. But think about this essential truth – had I not jumped down to those perilous rocks and encouraged others to do the same, Miss Darling would have had no one to rescue and would not have become so famous. But I bear no grudges, I again succeeded in surviving a catastrophe and, for the time being, lost any desire for public acclaim.

I made do with a pleasant night in the arms of the Ship's Carpenter before getting a coach down from Beadnells to Newcastle-upon Tyne, where I stayed for a few days. It was very grey. My experiences at sea having left me feeling quite remote from reality, I trudged round the city streets much as I had done in London after losing Harriet, barely conscious of my surroundings.

Even on the final part of my journey, I was totally oblivious of the driver of the Express Coach urging his horses to full tilt in his determination to break the record time between Darlington and York. It seems other passengers blamed him for throwing them around and rattling their teeth and led to the coachman being fined 40/- at York Magistrates Court. For my part, I harbour few concerns about coach travel but I can tell you here and now that I will never, ever go to sea again! Perhaps that newly fangled railway will have to satisfy the emergence of any future wanderlust.

Chapter 18

The Weddings of Mr. & Mrs. John Welburn and of Queen Victoria

Queen Victoria got married and became Mrs. Albert Saxe-Coburg Gotha although you cannot suppose she signed her letters in that way. Having Prince Albert on hand to discuss the matters of the day and the state must have been such a comfort.

Perhaps it was all the excitement about weddings that set me off thinking that if I really wanted a husband for myself then this was an opportune time to start looking. Now my own 'Mama' had passed away I was compelled to find my own man; not that she would have put herself out to find anyone to suit me. You may ask yourself why a successful and independent woman at my time of life should suddenly feel the need of a husband. The humdrum truth was, despite being property-owning and wealthy, marriage seemed the only way for me to attain respectability.

My plan to devise accidental encounters with an acceptable candidate involved ensuring I was always elegantly dressed and supremely poised when out and about. Initially I looked at members of the clergy but decided that to adopt religion seriously would prove too great a burden for me. No doubt any member of the legal or medical profession would consider me unsuitable so I decided to pursue one of my own kind, a shopkeeper. My own grocer's shop was doing well due to my intense application on becoming its legitimate owner but I left it to Mr. Carter to run it. I lived in the house next door and gave advice, whether or not he needed it.

It took a few years to identify a suitable widower in possession of a pleasant appearance and sufficient income; I had no wish to be bound to anyone who may regard my wealth my principal attraction. I persevered because at my age, with no expectations of being a heroine of a romantic encounter, I knew I could play the part of a supportive wife. As a single woman I had devoted a lot of hard work and enterprise to accumulating my money and of course marriage means all rights over a woman's land and property instantly becomes that of her husband. But as Mrs. Fitzherbert had once told me, 'Marriage to any rich old man is a judicious strategy for a woman.'

The gentleman I eventually decided upon was Mr. John Welburn who had a profitable family business near Sow Hill selling superior boots and shoes. He personified reliability with his resolute chin and moderate quantity of greying hair. I had a nodding acquaintance with him as he had lived further up Keldgate with his wife until she died; he'd then moved in with his elder sister in North Bar Within and rented out his old marital home, Albany House.

I bought more footwear than I had any legitimate need for, discussing the latest styles and colours and finicking about the fit with my intended. Eventually, whenever I entered his premises I noted, his face light up as if by sunshine. I put myself out to exchange the time of day with him in the street and got into the habit of attending his local church of St. Mary's rather than the Minster. Finding ourselves sitting next to each other at a talk at the Guild Hall given by Mr. Moses Roper, an escaped American slave, we got to talking about the unfairness of life. I don't believe Mr. W. had many friends so I learned a great deal about his family and his beliefs

After church one Sunday as Mr. Welburn walked me back to Keldgate and I asked him into my parlour to have a glass of sherry wine with me. I was rather proud of my neat new cellaret with discreetly confined wine bottles. Whether daytime alcohol or the fact that 1844 was a Leap Year played a part, I cannot tell you but I found unrehearsed words issuing from my mouth without notice.

'Mr. Welburn, we do seem to be getting on very amiably do you not think?'

'We certainly do Elizabeth, if I may call you by your given name. I do enjoy our conversations I certainly... Yes, yes, I certainly do.' Mr. Welburn ran his finger round his collar looking very uncertain.

Being doubtful whether Mr. Welburn would ever make a proposal I judged it would be better to make my intentions clear, 'It seems to me that it would be eminently sensible for us to wed and enjoy some comfort and companionship together for whatever time we have left to us. Is there any real reason for us to remain miserable and single?'

He seemed very surprised. He asked for time to consider the matter before leaving rather hastily. For several weeks we had no social contact during which time I constantly berated myself for my brashness and considered my plans to have been in vain. Then Lord bless us, one afternoon there was Mr. Welburn standing at the threshold holding his hat. My maid admitted him into the parlour where he made a formal proposal, proffering a very nice blue sapphire ring.

'I'm delighted to accept your proposal, sir and I promise to make myself unfailingly agreeable,' my exultant smile quite made my cheeks ache.

'Now Elizabeth, we will keep this to ourselves for a few months, so put away the ring safely for the time being. I need time to organise the business so that all the family are assured of some sort of income. Taking such a step at my time of life will come as quite a shock to them. Some may say it's an imprudent match but I know all will come to appreciate the stalwart woman you are,' said Mr. Welburn, firmly seizing both my hands.

What could I say? I wanted to tell the whole town that I had at last secured a husband, even at my advanced age but for the time being I must learn to hold my tongue in order to successfully take my place in the world as a 'stalwart woman'.

For months I drew up wedding plans, thought about clothes, food and guests; lists were constantly being made and discarded. Mr. W. told me nothing of the reaction of his family when he summoned up the strength to break the news of our betrothal; I sensed it was not gladly received. A short discreet notice was placed in the Hull Advertiser, Mr. Welburn gave his tenants notice to quit and we arranged to move into Albany House. My first outing as an affianced woman was when, on the arm of my freshly acquired fiancé, we attended the wedding of Mr. Richard Hodgson the tannery owner who celebrated his own special day with a substantial dinner at the Hall Garth Inn.

Needless to say, the occasion fired me up to make my own nuptials the more impressive. Mr. Welburn could have no objection to my arrangements because he had allowed me to pay for them. We also celebrated our marriage in the Minster, choir boys singing and bells ringing, before crossing Minster Yard over to the Hall Garth Inn. At last I felt confident in taking my place among the honourable matrons of Beverley.

Despite Mr. Straker being extremely efficient at organising wedding breakfasts on a large scale, I had insisted he brought in extra staff from the Black Bull in Lairgate which he also owned. I wished service to all the tables to be perfectly co-ordinated. And I had every one of his waiters fitted out in smart, matching waistcoats for them to keep afterward.

One of John's brothers had suggested a better venue would have been the Angel for one of Daniel Boyes 'far-famed' pies but I never have believed 'big' to be definitely better. When I think of that enormous one his pastry cook made at Christmas that weighed 10 stone and could feed about 40 people, it makes me nauseous. Just think how many grimy hands would have touched it. For my celebration at the Hall Garth Inn, I ensured chilled champagne was served with every course from the Mulligatawny soup, the meats and accompaniments through to the pastries and jellies. I stinted on nothing.

Most of the Welburn family had put aside their doubts about my doubtful reputation apart that is, from Mr. Welburn's two unmarried sisters who, having declared themselves staunchly against our match still put in an appearance for the feast. But being despised by your own sex should be regarded as a compliment don't you think? For several minutes, those two patronising and condescending women stood near the dining room doorway holding a pile of shawls despite the warmth of the day, glancing unsmilingly around the room. Ignoring their raw-boned antipathy, I welcomed them and, with conspicuous politeness, personally ushered them to their seats.

Would you not assume most sisters would be glad to see their brother happily married again? Perhaps there was a slight warming toward me on the part of the younger sister but the elder Miss Welburn remained frosty. She had a look of my husband but with a finer moustache. As he came across to greet her, she gave him a quick glance up and down, sniffed but made no comment on his handsome diamond shirt pin, my wedding gift to him. I had made certain my new husband would be as faultlessly appointed as I was myself on our wedding day. He'd presented me with a beautiful pair of soft kid boots which, I'd hinted, would admirably set off my sumptuous indigo silk and wool gown with lace collar and cuffs.

Miss Matilda Welburn need not have worried about being left destitute as Mr. Welburn was the most fair and business-like gentleman you could ever imagine. He was punctilious in ensuring everyone in his family had an assured income and now as my husband and responsible for my property, he also took care to be a punctilious landlord. He ensured repairs were properly done to the buildings at Weel and the land protected by regular inspection and repair to the banks of the River Hull. I was particularly pleased to find he had no objection to changing his will in my favour as Mrs. Fitzherbert had recommended so long ago. Such a considerate man.

It took me a considerably longer time to persuade Mr. Welburn that a visit to London would be an admirable diversion for us. He had little experience of travel before he met me, being too caught up with the family business. But I was beset by a whim to reacquaint myself with those far-off days when I'd wandered the streets with my perfidious friend Michael, not that I gave that as a reason for going. It was my suggestion of taking the railway train to make our expedition even more memorable that swung Mr. W. to my way of thinking.

Mr. Welburn was at pains to assure me that everyone soon got used to the speed of this new mode of transport and there was nothing whatsoever for me to be concerned about. Having survived a carriage crash, two fires and a shipwreck, I was convinced I would have no qualms about rail travel. But as my fearless husband saw his duty was to provide reassurance, I acted the part of the timorous wife and dutifully thanked him for his counsel.

His authority on the matter of trains came from being one of the nine hundred guests invited to the official opening of the Hull to Bridlington railway line two years ago. Three engines had towed them all sitting in sixty-six carriages to eat a huge lunch at Bridlington in the goods station, take a walk along the promenade in an invigorating breeze before returning to Hull for yet another blow-out. Every man who had worked on the project received bread, cheese and beer.

For those not important enough to ride in the trains, grand celebrations were arranged at stops along the line in order to bring reassurance to all those distrustful of rail travel of whom there were many. Even before the line was in proper use, one railway man had his head crushed against the buffers and a train broke the leg of another.

In Beverley a general holiday had enabled hundreds of people including myself, to venture up to the Trinities to the new elegant station building. The Council had sold the site to the railway company for £400 creating a general belief that rail tracks heralded ever more economic advances for the town. I caught a glimpse of Mr. George Hudson himself. How disappointing to observe this so-called 'Railway King' being so short of stature with a prominent paunch and eyes that operated at variance to each other. Thomas Carlyle called him a 'big swollen gambler', but I'll tell you a lot more about him later.

A new hostelry in the Station Square named 'The Telegraph' was thriftily built using materials rescued from the demolition of the Lairgate Theatre. Merely the colour of those distinctive gault bricks sparked memories of that crucial morning when I had closed Mam's back door behind me and joined the theatre all those years ago. How can I be that same person? I laugh to myself when I think of how nervous I was then of making my first long coach journey with strangers.

So why would I be nervous of a railway journey now? For one thing, I was with my husband and for another, hadn't a thousand people from Beverley travelled safely to the Hull Fair and back on the railway last year? Alas, my heart confounded me by churning alarmingly the first time I actually stepped on to a railway train. Once I'd accustomed myself to the clangour of the engine and the countryside chasing past, I settled back, glancing through the window at cattle fleeing away from the unaccustomed noise and children waving from the side of track. I waved back, more regal I'm sure than our dear Queen in her Royal Train; she insisted on ringing a bell to signal her driver to slow down whenever she believed he was speeding recklessly.

Arriving at Kingston upon Hull we stepped out on to Paragon Station. I was astounded to see hundreds of navvies digging deep to prepare the ground for the largest Station Hotel in the whole country in anticipation of the hundreds of visitors expected to flock into Hull.

Mr. Welburn hailed a porter who conducted us to a train bound for Selby. To get there we had to pass over a most peculiar bridge which Mr. W. said was called a bascule. It parted in the middle and raised the rail track up like two arms whenever barges and ships needed to come through. Railway passengers must sit in their carriages patiently waiting for the rails to be lined up again for the train to proceed. Despite this performance it took but a couple of hours to get to the George for our dinner. Then there we were, off steaming away down to London in less time than you could have believed possible.

Looking back, I reckon I actually had more fun there with Michael. Until I got to know him for the bounder he was, I'd enjoyed our walks, exploring the little lanes and riverside paths for hours. He would tell me magical stories about the people and places. Of course, you couldn't believe half of them. But walking with my Mr. Welburn, we were obliged to find a seat at regular intervals so he could get his breath. He wasn't nearly as impressed with London as I'd hoped. The hurrying and scurrying and the price of everything, particularly of the shoes and boots, were not to his liking. Above all it was the London noise that he complained about. At times I did wonder whether I'd selected the wrong husband after all.

Contrarily it was the noise of a big city that I missed in Beverley. There you look out whenever you catch the rumble of a cart or a dray passing, just to see what's going on. Noise carries on in London unceasingly, day and night. Hawkers, Hackney carriages, horses and hooligans, cries from newsmen, muffin men and milkmen mingle with pattens clinking on stone setts.

Even after we'd decided on our excursion, we still had long debates about the wisdom of visiting London mostly because Mr. Welburn fretted about the unrest arising from the Chartist Rally earlier in the year. Eventually I convinced Mr. Welburn of the need to seize every opportunity to enjoy life in whatever time we had left.

We stayed in a select hotel, saw all the sights like Buckingham Palace, Hyde Park and the Tower of London. We joined the crowds gathered to see the newly attached bronze plaque at the base of Nelson's impressively tall Column; Mr. W. was keen to inform me it commemorated the Battle of the Nile where our heroic Admiral lost his eye.

After often vaunting my desire for new experiences, Mr. Welburn accused me of being completely irrational for declining his suggestion for a cruise on the Thames down to Greenwich. My tragic adventure on board the SS Forfarshire I'd kept to myself. Erasing it from memory was impossible particularly when the paddle steamer 'Pegasus' went down five years ago on its way to Hull drowning seventy people. My remedy for misery and misfortune has habitually been to ignore it and displace it with something else. This time I had no option but to tell Mr. W. the full story.

So instead of a boat ride we sat and talked about the shipwreck, looking across the River Thames towards the South Bank. We planned to cross the bridge to have a look at Kennington Common. In April, 25,000 Chartists had assembled there prior to their proposed march across Westminster Bridge to Parliament with an enormous petition. It bore six million unlikely signatures including several by Queen Victoria, the Duke of Wellington and Mr. Punch.

The Chartists were outraged when thousands of Special Constables prevented anyone crossing to the north bank except for their leader.

Having hailed a Hansom cab, the driver refused to go south of the river, describing it as a grassless place full of black ditches and a vitriol factory emitting stinking fumes.   On reflection we decided to remain sitting on our bench and progress to a discussion of the principles of Chartism.   In his role of Prison Visitor, Mr. Welburn had visited Robert Peddie, a Chartist imprisoned in the House of Correction for three years hard labour who opined Beverley was a 'Whig hellhole.' His poem 'A Voice from Beverley' begins, 'Hark the doleful prison bell, resounding through my dreary cell'. He was good at rhymes.

Mr. Welburn pronounced the Chartist Movement incapable of succeeding because everyone knows the lower classes have no clout; this I thought was a shameful betrayal.   Surely Mr. Welburn should definitely be on their side because of their belief in a good education for everybody.   The ability to read and write brings opportunities to earn more, and, therefore, the ability to buy more from shops such as his.   Mr. W was not used to being contradicted and made the point that whoever was in charge of a country would look after their own first and the commonalty just had to lump it. To avoid getting into further political argument and as we were nearby, I suggested a stroll to take in a view of the Houses of Parliament.

'You seem to know your way round here very well Elizabeth', said my new husband.

'Of course I do.   I would come here every week when I was housekeeping for Mr. Bellingham,' said I, quite without thinking.

Mr. W. darted a sharp glance at my face, 'Who d'you say? John Bellingham do you mean?   But that's the name of ...'

'Yes', I said, 'that's the one.   We'd come down here regularly just so he could present his petition so everyone was used to him being there and nodded him through. I often went with him just to have a look round.'

'Why have you never thought to mention this to me before, Elizabeth? I find it very strange I must say.' Mr. W. was staring hard at me as if he could not believe he knew me.

'Why John, I really didn't think you would be interested in something that occurred so many years before we met. It's as if it were another life.' I tried my best to make light of the matter, patting his hand. I'd forgotten that wild oats had never been sown in his youth what with him being so committed to the family business.

'Well it so happens that I am very interested. I mean to say, it's only five years ago that Robert Peel's secretary was shot dead here in the street in mistake for him. London's a dangerous place, I've always thought so and we should never have come. But I do feel I should know more about what you call your other life down here and all that time you spent away from Beverley.'

'As you wish, John, if it will make you happy. I suppose I used to enjoy that feeling of standing where history happens. And the House of Commons; I'm so glad that it's still standing here beside the Thames. King William was all for moving it to Buckingham House after the Great Fire you know. I would come here with Mr. Bellingham to ask for compensation for being put in prison while carrying out the orders of the Foreign Minister. He got cross when people just nodded and said they'd see what could be done but nothing ever was.'

I left it at that, diverting him by pointing out the joy of several urchins watching a Punch and Judy Show, while others danced round a boy playing a barrel organ. To reveal that the last time I'd been in London, by innocently feeding a furnace with faggots I had occasioned the burning of the House of Commons would never have relighted our conjugal bliss. Particularly with Welburn as my surname, I felt it behoved me to keep that spark of information securely under a bushel.

Chapter 19

The Railway King

We got a Hansom back to our hotel. Mr. Welburn fulminated against the cost for some time. Later apologising for his ill-humour, which he blamed upon his state of utter weariness. To make amends and to commemorate our London divertissement he bought me a framed print by an artist named Turner; ironically the subject was the burning of the House of Commons. I summoned up all my theatrical skills to convincingly express my surprise and delight to my husband whilst inwardly appalled to be forced to recall that tragic evening all those years ago.

The following day we took the train home to Yorkshire and by then Mr. Welburn's doubts about my chequered past seemed to have moderated. The prospect of home comforts put him in distinctly better spirits. For the first time during our acquaintance, he demonstrated a quiet drollery that previously I'd had no reason to suspect he possessed as he started telling me something of his own escapades.

'You know Elizabeth, sitting here like this in a railway carriage puts me in mind of that trip up to Bridlington and back when they opened the railway line through Beverley. That was a day to remember and no mistake,' he said. 'You would not believe the quantity of spirits we got through.'

'Oh yes', I chaffed him, 'it was alright for the likes of men of consequence like you Mr. Welburn, snug in the carriage with all the great and the good. What about us poor spectators getting soaked to the very skin? With no refreshments whatsoever I might add.'

He laughed, 'Don't know about that my dear, but I certainly found myself sitting next to a very great, very fat man and from what he told me of his business, he certainly could not claim to be good.'

'Whoever was that? He sounds like an interesting gentleman.'

'Why it was Mr. George Hudson himself! Some call him the 'Railway King'. I've never in my life seen anyone who could put away so much drink and still speak. In fact, he never stopped talking throughout the whole journey. He makes it his business to let everyone know he associates with all the right people like the Duke of Devonshire and the Duke of Carlisle.'

'I too am acquainted with the Duke of Carlisle's wife, Georgiana,' I informed him, instinctively boasting while stupidly forgetting my resolution to say nothing of my former life.

'Do you indeed? Well, there's something else of your past of which I know nothing at all,' remarked Mr. Welburn, again looking discomfited.

'Oh, I met her at Castle Howard, years ago,' I said in an offhand manner. 'But I want you to tell me more about Mr. Hudson. I must say he didn't look very impressive to me when I saw him through the rain, but then nor did I.'

'No, I suppose at first glance no one would ever believe him to be one of the most successful railway proprietors in the whole country. Shall I tell you how he can afford to buy a house in Knightsbridge and entertain luminaries like Prince Albert and the Duke of Wellington?'

'I heard he'd inherited a lot of money from an aged relative. Some say staying with his dying uncle, night and day for weeks ensured he was the main legatee to the family fortune.'

'Oh, any man in his position is bound to attract ugly rumours. But what he told me was straight from the horse's mouth so to speak. And 'In vino veritas' he could not help but crow about controlling a quarter of all the railway networks in this country. I asked him how he managed to achieve so much in so short a time and that opened the floodgates. Of course it was purely down to his shrewdness and business acumen! He bought up country estates like that one he bought from the Duke of Devonshire near Market Weighton. A clever move on his part because it was the best land for a direct railway line from York to Beverley. I wished I'd never asked.'

'Of course! I did wonder why he wanted to live out there, well away from anywhere,' I said.

'I know, everyone said the same, but his idea was that once he owned that land, no other rail company but his could build on it. And not only that, all compensation due from the agreement went straight into his own pocket and not his company's. But what really tickled his fancy was that his sons were able to come home from Pocklington School on his train travelling along his own railway line, get off at his own private station, and into a waiting carriage and be back with their mother at Londesborough Hall in no time at all.'

'I did wonder why Mr. Hudson was prepared to pay the Duke of Devonshire £470,000 for his estate. You could buy Beverley for that.' The amount of power money gives to people always impresses me.

'To be quite honest with you, I felt all his money must have gone to his head along with all that alcohol. His riches persuaded him he could do absolutely anything he wished and I, as a fellow businessman should applaud his enterprise. He'd been selling land he didn't own to various rail companies and strictly against the law, he'd paid dividends to his shareholders from capital and not from his revenue. Honestly, he told me almost every particular of his improper business strategy yet I would hazard right now he has not one notion of anything he confided to an absolute stranger.'

'How fascinating! But I will applaud him for his energy. Only look what he's wrought in so short a time. Everyone is travelling by railway train now; it's no wonder he's proud of himself,' I said.

'Now you must promise me Elizabeth that not one word of what I've told you will ever be repeated to anyone. Mr. Hudson is not the type of gentleman who would scruple to bring a charge of slander against any person he believed had maligned him.'

'Why Mr. Welburn, by now you should know I'm the soul of discretion. There is absolutely no possibility of me telling anyone what you have just told me,' I said. And, as you know, I never break my word.

Alighting from the train in Beverley that evening, we were bewildered to find people ranged along Grovehill Lane scooping up black treacle from the paving stones. A cask had fallen while being loaded from a goods train on to a cart. With pots and spoons most of the sticky stuff was removed from the setts and spread onto bread, grittier than usual. As ever, Beverley folk let nothing go to waste.

The uneventful yet comfortable rhythm of married life was not exactly what I'd had in mind when setting my bonnet at Mr. Westoby; in fact it was rather boring. Rather than coming straight out with a proposal to visit London again because of his proclaimed dislike of the place, I thought to insinuate the idea into my husband's brain by subtle hints every few months or so.

I would say, 'Mr. Westoby, now we have the speed and comfort of the railway why should we not take a trip every year?' or 'How delightful it would be to see that Jewel Cabinet that Prince Albert had given his bride although of course, no wedding present could compare with my beautiful kid boots'. I suggested making a visit to the King's Library in the British Museum, to see King George III's collection of thousands of books, donated by his son, who, you would suspect, never had occasion to open a book himself. I prattled on, 'How did we ever endure day after day in a stage coach down to London? By railway it is now so effortless; how could we bear to miss the Great Exhibition?' This proved to be the categorical last straw.

How was I to know my proposition would coincide with Mr. Welburn returning home after an unfortunate encounter with Gillyatt Sumner? As one of the first visitors to the Great Exhibition, Gilly felt a compulsion to let everyone know his observations on the scale and splendour of the event. His obsession had actually begun a few years earlier when a famous sculptor proposed to make a cast of our ancient Percy Shrine in the Minster and put it on public display at the Crystal Palace in 1851. He wished to 're-produce the whole monument as probably the most beautiful specimen of purely English design which has remained in a fair state of preservation.'

Mr. Sumner was outraged when he discovered he'd been excluded from all official discussions and first heard of the matter in a newspaper. As, in his words, being a 'respected antiquarian', Gilly issued a Notice bewailing "the DISGRACE of being the only place in the World that has refused to contribute to that Museum of the World The New Crystal Palace that has for its object the Social, Moral and Intellectual Advancement of the great masses of the People."

Gillyatt took the whole matter personally and began a vicious quarrel with Reverend Birtwhistle, as he and the St. Martins Churchwardens had refused downright to countenance the project. And after having personally witnessed the unparalleled wonders of industry and culture at the Great Exhibition, he felt an evangelical urge to justify his opinion to everyone including my husband. Mr. Welburn was irritated beyond measure at being constrained to listen to such an interminable soliloquy. In common with so many others, he was ready to be prejudiced against anything commended by Gillyatt Sumner.

Stock still in the parlour, Mr. W. declared he wouldn't be seen dead at the Great Exhibition and if he never saw London again, he wouldn't give a tinker's cuss. Furthermore, he ranted, if he had listened to me and we'd gone down there the year after our honeymoon we would have surely caught the Cholera because no one knew they had it until it was too late and you could barely breathe there because of the lime they used to clean the air. He went on and on citing a hundred reasons why he would never ever leave Yorkshire again.

I was genuinely taken aback by just how badly I had misjudged the strength of Mr. Welburn's opposition to my plan. Pa used to tell Mam she should never push him too far because there is no anger quite like that of a quiet man; I should have taken heed. Utterly routed by his displeasure I was wary for several days. To avoid any possible source of discord I made sure the household ran smoothly and even played cribbage with my husband every evening. At all events I was determined to have a successful if tedious marriage if only to prove his insufferable sisters wrong in their assessment of me.

I'm sure you must be wondering how my devoted husband chose to make amends for his choler. One morning, observing him toing and froing in the garden, smoking his favoured cigar, the notion that he was coming to regret our union crept into my mind. But no, it turned out that he was deciding that the most excellent way to make his dear wife happy, was to hire a gig to the Corporation Pier in Hull to witness Queen Victoria's first visit to East Yorkshire. As you know, I have never been one to complain so I subdued my Republican tendencies and played the part of the grateful wife.

Having laid claim to a bench, we sat for hours waiting for the Royal Party to come and wave at us after ceremoniously opening the Philosophical and Literary Society Building which enabled the insertion of 'Royal' before the rest of its title. Along with hundreds of excited Hull folk we watched the Queen being assisted from her carriage. How we cheered as she knighted Mayor Henry Cooper by tapping him on the shoulders with a ceremonial sword right out there on the breezy pier which became the 'Victoria Pier' the very next day.

The Royal Yacht 'Fairy' took the Royal party across the estuary to enjoy Grimsby. Mr. Welburn's uncustomary profligacy continued into the evening when I found he had paid £1. 5s for two tickets to a special dinner put on by Hull Corporation. This was more to my liking.

Since I first decided to marry him, I relied upon my acting ability to convince Mr. Welburn that I believed him to be handsome, virile and wise. I strove to be the wife he wished for and kept all household accounts scrupulously. He understood about Harriet and laid the entire blame for my situation on Mr. Fox. At no time did I tell him about my theatrical ventures or my part in the Great Stock Exchange Fraud being convinced such enterprises would shock his religious scruples. I did not wish to go into details of the duel between George Canning and Lord Castlereagh as I would surely have been quizzed about the reason I was there. Nor did I give him a full account of my time with John Bellingham or with

Henry Hunt. My discretion worked a treat, for Mr. Welburn defended me against the world and gave me everything I'd ever wished for – status and security.

Chapter 20

Where the Blame Really Lies

I nurtured the belief that the best way to deal with my husband's sensibilities was to ensure he would remain in ignorance of my past. As he has now departed from this life, I have decided this day is the most propitious time to disclose more of my story to you and thereby clear my mind.

As a 'dowager' I am entitled to regain my legal existence and therefore my property in Weel village as well as Mr. Welburn's estate which includes several houses he rented out in the town, all bringing me a substantial income. I have Albany House to myself without the dominion of a man and, without actually gloating, I like to welcome people to my home. The house is quite grand compared to many of the other houses on Keldgate with a nice bit of land at the back. I'll show you around if you have a few minutes to spare.

Albany House was the home of Mr. Welburn and his first wife and much of the furniture was her choice. I didn't really share her taste so I've been re-arranging things and buying new just because I can and also, it's something to occupy me, now I'm on my own.

Up on the top floor is where my new live-in maid, Becky has her own bedroom and sitting room. She's pleased as Punch to have so much space to herself instead of how she was at her Mam's with six brothers and sisters in a two-up two-down. I looked at quite a few lasses before deciding on her; she keeps me informed about what's going on in the town and she's good with my hair.

Then here on the first floor there's the bedroom Mr. Welburn shared with his wife in that big white bed. I didn't fancy sleeping there but I go in sometimes to rearrange the tiny furniture in Harriet's baby house that Mr. Fox paid a joiner to make for her years ago. I brought it with me and set it up on a chest of drawers. I'm enjoying my second childhood; my first one had little in the way of frippery. The first Mrs. W. must have bought that little model of a guillotine; it looks out of place next to the dolls' house I know, but when I think how some French Prisoner of War spent hours carving it out of mutton bones, I couldn't just throw it out.

The first Mrs. Welburn had chosen the bedroom at the back of the house being a light sleeper and on Keldgate carts rattle along from early morning. But me, I'm quite the opposite. I like the street noise I can hear in my bedchamber at the front. I sometimes stand up here at the window with Becky and she tells me tales of all the people passing by. It makes me feel more part of the fabric of the town, yet as ever still on the edge of other people's lives. There's my dressing room next door but most of my clothes I have stored in the small bedroom. There's not much bustling from milliner to draper now.

I go into the small bedroom every now and again to check for dust and cobwebs then chivvy Becky into running a duster over everything. Now is probably the time to get rid of some my clutter. Let's have a good look round to see what I can give to the Charity for the Relief of Poor Widows. That chest of drawers belonged to the first Mrs. Welburn and clothes like my favourite Spencer Jacket are folded away in there. I can't get into it now but no, I can't bring myself to get rid. Did you know that Spencer Jackets were named after Earl Spencer whose habit of standing in front of his fireplace caused him to burn his coat tails so he had them cut off? Like me he didn't like throwing away good clothes.

Gowns that I'd once found so desirable and flattering are now so old-fashioned; what could I have been thinking when I bought them? I suppose back then I was easily taken in by assurances from shop folks praising my taste and discernment. Some clever seamstress will be able to make something from the fabric I have no doubt. I'll pull some out and leave Becky to see to them.

There's our Bill's footstool pushed under a dressing table. I'll have to keep that, even if it does put me in mind of Amy. She's gone now. But he's still my dependable brother and we get along quite well. And in the wide bottom drawer there's Harriet's collections of stones and shells carefully spread out; I'd put some of the prettiest ones in her coffin.

I got Bill's son James to come across and hang some pictures for me in here to make it look more homely. He's an obliging lad, a lot cleverer than his pa. When I was Hannah Murphy, I did have my portrait painted once by Mr. Harlow, but it probably got destroyed in the Drury Lane fire. I've still got that print of Parliament in flames that Mr. Westoby bought in London. It's strange to think of that artist, Mr. Turner, who would have been hurrying toward the House of Commons to sketch it burning while I was doing my best to get as far away as possible from the wretched place.

I'm not sure I'm pronouncing it correctly but that lithograph of 'L'Assemble Nationale' opposite the window is one I'd bought because at the time it was first published, the Prince Regent was so infuriated at the way he was portrayed as a corpulent buffoon, he paid a fortune to bribe the printmaker to destroy the original plate. As Queen Caroline once said 'He was very fat and nothing like as handsome as his portrait'. Prinny's bribe was accepted but to everyone's glee the printing plate later emerged unscathed from its hiding place and hundreds of prints of the cartoon were put on sale. On close inspection you can see Mr. James Gillray has drawn several members of the Devonshire family as well as Mrs. Fitz Herbert and even my dear Mr. Sheridan.

Next to it there's that print of St. Peter's Fields. I don't often look at it in spite of me being depicted there, standing on a rully in my stylish white dress, waving that huge banner. You'll remember how I left it at the Bull and Mouth in Leeds as it was so filthy after all the brawling and upset. Everyone assumed the Yeomanry had just charged straight into the crowd from sheer stupidity. But the fact of the matter was that when that Hussar motioned me to pick up the trumpet he'd dropped on the ground, I fully intended to hand it straight back to him. The excitement of the moment and the highest of spirits seduced me into blowing into it just as hard as I could.

Had I time to reflect, I may have recalled the occasion in Wiltshire when that young fellow had blown the coachman's horn so loudly it caused the horses to bolt and the coach to turn over. Why did It not occur to me that a sudden blast near its ears would cause the soldier's mount to rear up and him to lose his grip on the reins, and cling round the horse's neck as it dashed amuck into the mob? How could I know that on seeing the Hussar stranded in the centre of a menacing crowd the rest of the Yeomanry would charge into them like madmen? The screams and shouts quite drowned out the clatter the trumpet made when I dashed it to the ground double quick.

My time spent with Mr. Hunt meant a lot to me and to my unremitting shame I must acknowledge to you that it was my thoughtless action which was to blame for all the damage and deaths occurring that day as well as for Mr. Hunt's two-years of misery in gaol.

Anyway, let's not dwell on that shameful period of my life. We'll go down to the lower regions of the house and I'll ring for Becky to bring tea to the drawing room. While we're waiting, I'll tell you a bit about my part in the disgrace of George Hudson, the Railway King; I know you are longing to know. Well, as you are aware, my cousin Robert was on good terms with Mr. George Leeman, that fellow who was Lord Mayor of York three times. What had really riled Mr. Leeman was George Hudson promising his York and North Midland Railway Company would pay £30,000 to build Lendal Bridge over the river Ouse in the city centre before mendaciously backing out of the arrangement. Mr. Leeman emphatically disagreed with any public funds being used for the building of the bridge because, as he said, it was planned purely for the benefit of Mr. Hudson and his business.

Cousin Robert had told me Mr. Leeman was desperate to find positive proof of George Hudson's criminality and bring him to face justice in the Courts. So where did I go the day after we arrived back in Beverley after our London excursion? Why straight round to Robert Taylor's grocery shop in Saturday Market and disclosed to him everything that Mr. Welburn had told me about his conversation on the train with George Hudson when pickled to the gills. I do have a tendency to exaggerate and perhaps I did add a bit to Mr. W.'s account nevertheless, Mr. Leeman soon received a long letter from my cousin for which he was very grateful.

By the following year Mr. Hudson had to sell all his country estates and pay some of the costs of Lendal Bridge. Being Member of Parliament for Sunderland, he couldn't be prosecuted for debt but he's packed that in now and he's supposed to be trying to pay everyone back. If he doesn't, he'll certainly end up in gaol. Despite promising my husband to tell no one of the matter, you surely must commend me for doing my civic duty in exposing Mr. Hudson's chicanery. It is to be hoped that now some may get their money back and, I devoutly pray, he will never discover who is really to blame for his downfall.

While Becky clears away the tea things, we'll go across the hall to Mr. Welburn's study. His desk is where I tend to put things like old accounts and letters. Let's have a look in this drawer. You see, I've kept all Harriet's letters, tied up in ribbon - some addressed to me and some to Rev. Coltman that he'd passed on to me.

And in the drawer below, there are calling cards from people like Lady Georgiana and Mrs. Fitzherbert. I've kept theatre programmes of plays I'd appeared in years ago like 'Everyone has his Faults', played every night to a full house throughout the hottest summer imaginable. Amazingly I find I can still recall some of the lines and the strain it took to deliver them above the clamour of the Pit. Sadly, now for the life of me I cannot even bring to mind the name of the lady who lives next door.

Oh yes, there's that official letter I've left out, still sitting on the writing slope. I received that about two years ago summoning me to London to give evidence of 'electoral bribery' of all things. I really didn't fancy going back down there again on my own. It's from some government body ordering me to appear before a committee to give a statement about our Robert's involvement in the goings-on at past elections. There's really nothing I can add to their decision that civic rule in Beverley was 'feeble, careless and extravagant' because it still is.

I know for a fact that any commissioner worth his salt would soon worm it out of me how I'd been responsible for knocking folk out by putting laudanum into teapots, so I've decided to ignore the summons and nothing has transpired as yet. Surely, they wouldn't put an old woman into a gaol would they? The strange thing is, what they call a transgression was something I hadn't even regarded as wrong. Why would I? In the past the opposing parties had always agreed to ignore any so-called 'breach of ethics.' It's only just recently they've begun accusing each other of all sorts of skullduggery. I actually feel more guilt about accidentally setting fire to the House of Commons than merely meddling with elections.

Mr. Welburn's study is much as he left it really. Books are all neatly arranged in alphabetical order and that stack of notebooks is where he would meticulously record his day-by-day activities. They are rather dull. Mr. Fox's books are in the big bookcase in the back parlour, I'd hate to throw any of them out. Someone will clear the house when I'm in my own wooden box and wonder about him when they see his name written on the flyleaf; he signed every single one of his books.

There's a secret compartment in the Davenport that Mr. Welburn showed me how to open. I won't show you exactly where it is but you have to be able to locate a tiny ridge on the back panel and press hard. I can't bend down to it now but I do know what I hid in there soon after I moved in. It's the fifty calibre pistol my father taught me to shoot so he could to explain to me how James Hadfield should have shot King George III.

Now I wish to interrupt any further tour of my house in order to confess to you what is probably the very worst thing I have ever done. It occurred when I was only 26 years old but I will not use that as an excuse. Among my other 'souvenirs' hidden with the pistol is a fifty-year old newspaper which describes a certain event.

As everyone knows, our Prime Minister, Mr. Spencer Percival was shot on 11th May, 1812 in the House of Commons lobby at 5.15 p.m. And you will be aware I'd regularly gone there with Mr. Bellingham at his request; we looked like an everyday couple intending no harm to anyone. This one particular day, we'd dressed soberly and set off to Westminster in the middle of the afternoon. The parting in his hair had been getting wider so he'd started carefully combing it all forward.

Mr. Bellingham kept getting up and wandering about the lobby, consulting his watch until the Commons Chamber emptied as the Doorkeepers shouted 'Who goes home?' The Speaker had informed the Serjeant at Arms that the House would sit again the following morning at 10.30. Everything appeared as it should be as several Members came out and stood around chatting with Mr. Percival.

In my newspaper there is no reference to the woman beside John Bellingham who watched as his hand went to his pocket several times but came out empty. To my mind he'd plainly lost his nerve and would surely come to regret his cowardice. Without a thought I thrust my hand into that pocket I'd painstakingly sewn into his coat, seizing hold of the pistol I knew was there. Aiming, firing and pressing the weapon into Mr. Bellingham's limp grasp took seconds. The loud report had made me jump out of my skin but my acting prowess really came into its own when I slipped into the role of alarmed bystander. Quite calmly Mr. B. peered down at the gun in his hand then looked straight into the eyes of the Sergeant at Arms, saying 'I am the man that killed Mr. Percival.'

I reasoned It would have been wrong to deprive him of the infamy he craved; he may have been ashamed to admit that he didn't have the guts to carry out his plan. I don't think he was mad, just very annoyed. Some still say he should have been canonized for what he did.

And all those who rushed to arrest and imprison him, how badly would they have felt to have been shown to be so mistaken? No, it was far better to let him take the blame. I calmly left the House of Commons leaning on the arm of a considerate and kindly gentleman.

So there we are.

About the Author

Val Wise was born in Hull and has lived the majority of her life in Beverley, East Yorkshire. She has a huge passion for local history, art and her home town, which encouraged her to pursue a degree in history following retirement. Val worked as a nursery teacher for the majority of her life. She now enjoys a busy retirement, volunteering at the local theatre. Val's passion for local history has led her to regularly lead local history talks and walks and research work for the Beverley Guildhall's programme of exhibitions. 'The Blame Lies' is her third published book.

Also By Val Wise

FICTION

The Wrongs of Women

A novel based on Mary Wollstonecraft's early life in Beverley.
Available on Kindle/Paperback Amazon Publishing

NON-FICTION

Frederick Elwell R. A., 1870 – 1958

Available on Ebay/Online shops

Printed in Great Britain
by Amazon

70251515R00098